"I am asking you… marry me, Louise."

He was utterly mad. They had known each other less than a week. But Tom was looking at her, unsmiling, waiting for her answer. She could see that he was serious about his proposal.

What answer could she possibly give? He was still a stranger; there was so much that she didn't know about him. Did he love her?

And then she said, "Yes," and it was as if someone else had spoken in her place. She had never been impulsive, but she loved this man with all her heart. In spite of her misgivings, she said it again. "Yes, I will marry you."

OTHER
Harlequin Romances
by JANE DONNELLY

Many of these titles are available at your local bookseller
or through the Harlequin Reader Service.

For a free catalogue listing all available Harlequin Romances,
send your name and address to:

HARLEQUIN READER SERVICE,
M.P.O. Box 707, Niagara Falls, N.Y. 14302
Canadian address: Stratford, Ontario, Canada N5A 6W2

Love for a Stranger

by

JANE DONNELLY

Harlequin Books

TORONTO • LONDON • NEW YORK • AMSTERDAM
SYDNEY • HAMBURG • PARIS

Original hardcover edition published in 1978
by Mills & Boon Limited

ISBN 0-373-02195-X

Harlequin edition published September 1978

PRINTED IN U.S.A.

CHAPTER ONE

LOUISE LATHAM managed to park her van in the space behind the flats, and to walk upstairs to her bachelor girl apartment, meeting no one. She was glad she met no one.

In the bedroom cases were open, holiday clothes and accessories showed that the destination of the cases was somewhere in the sun. There was beachwear in an orderly pile on the bed, the dresses lying beside it were silken or cotton, and most of the clothes were new.

It wasn't a trousseau, but she had been certain that some time during this holiday in Spain Barry would ask her to marry him. The bedroom door was ajar and she closed it now, shutting out the feeling of happy anticipation that was in that room.

The living room was all pale muted colours. It was small but designed so that the illusion was spacious. Everything in here had been selected as suitable background for an up-and-coming interior decorator. Everything was functional and beautiful, and she stood with her back to the bedroom door feeling the tears start.

She wanted to howl aloud, to beat something with her fists, but she couldn't weep like that. Only quietly, sitting in one of the white modern chairs, her hands clenched, fighting to keep her sobs soundless, although there was no one to see or to hear her.

She hadn't cried for a long time. But just about ten minutes ago her world had collapsed.

She should have been leaving for Spain tomorrow. She and Barry should have been joining friends who had a holiday villa in Denia, and there was this understanding that while they were away they would plan their future together, Louise and Barry.

He had told her he wanted to propose to her in a romantic spot. They would have bought rings, perhaps, and there would have been a celebration, the four of them in the villa, toasting each other in the local wine, cooking a special meal.

She should have been having lunch with Barry now, and she had gone along to his office, in the square of the Northern town where she lived, to collect him. He was a builder; Barry Mason was a good name for a builder, up-and-coming like she was, except that he'd had the family firm to begin with.

He had been at his desk, going through papers, when she'd walked in, and he was big and blond and handsome and she knew how lucky she was: because she wasn't beautiful, she wasn't even pretty.

She was a girl who had always been too tall and too thin. Not slender, thin. The high cheekbones gave her hollow cheeks in a pointed face. Her wrists were bony, and she had salt-cellar hollows above and beneath her collarbone. She had been gawky and gangling until she'd learned how to move less self-consciously. Now, at least, her movements had grace, but Barry was handsome and Louise wasn't the only one who wondered what he saw in her.

'Sit down, sweetheart,' he'd said, and he'd gone on turning over the papers and scowling.

'Trouble?' she'd asked. There was always trouble in the building trade. He usually said,

'Flaming red tape,' or something like that. Today he said, 'This next job of yours, the big one, can you get an advance from them?'

She sat on a stool, her handbag on her knees. It was a tan leather bag with a shoulder strap, a sensible size for a sensible girl. Her shoes were tan leather too.

Large shoes for large feet, narrow large feet which made them even harder to fit.

'Yes for materials,' she said. 'What do you mean?'

He'd spoken as though it was obvious what he meant. 'I mean will they pay you now? You'll be starting on it as soon as we get back, so will they fork out beforehand?'

'No.' She was beginning to make a small name for herself, and this was her biggest chance yet. She wasn't going cap in hand, pleading poverty, it would have been very bad for her image. Besides, the glamorous blonde actress who was employing her might be famous for wide-eyed unsophisticated roles, but she wasn't the sort to pay for much in advance. Miss Paula Cavel was a tight-fisted lady, and Louise would have hated to ask her for any favours.

'Not a chance,' she said.

'You could try.'

'There isn't time, we're going on holiday tomorrow.' That wasn't the real reason, but it was another excuse until Barry said,

'We could take a later flight.'

'No. Anyhow, what difference can a few months make?'

He was taking it for granted that she would put her profits into his firm. She had been investing most of the money she had earned with Barry Mason, builder, for twelve months.

She had left the books-and-business side of it to him, she had trusted him. He was the sort of man everyone trusted—boyish-looking and happy.

'We need it now,' Barry had said. 'That's the difference. We're nearly bankrupt.'

He'd said that before. Business men were saying that all the time. She'd said, 'I can't,' wishing she could, but sure he would understand. 'She wouldn't pay out more than the minimum in advance. She really wouldn't. I've told you how she is. And it would be bad tactics to ask. The account's as safe as the Bank of England. She's a top-line star and her man's a millionaire, but I can't go asking her to pay before I even start the work.'

He looked at her with eyes that seemed flat and cold, as though he didn't want her to see through them, like blinds drawn down. She had seen that look in a man's eyes before. She recognised it as greed, anger and disappointment. She wanted to say, 'I'll try', so that he would blink away the shuttered look and smile at her.

She had never quarrelled with Barry. She had known him by sight most of her life. For the last eighteen months they had had what seemed a close and loving relationship, and they had never quarrelled. But now she had to go on, to strip their relationship down to the truth.

She said, 'I won't have had much return for my money, will I? All I've done is pay in.'

'You'll get it back.' He sounded impatient. 'You know you will.' His tone was wheedling, but he was flushed.

'If you don't go bankrupt first?'

He didn't care for the calm way she was saying that. 'Yes,' he snapped, and Louise knew that the quarrel was coming. She had never been able to handle discord. She always drew back from situations that looked like blowing up into a row, but there was no drawing back from this one.

She had been a fool about the money. It hadn't been a fortune, she wasn't in the big time yet, and at twenty-two her best years must be ahead. She had been in business, as an interior decorator-designer, on her own account for two years. This last year she had kept what she needed to live on, invested the rest in Barry's firm, and done cut price jobs for Barry's customers.

And just now Barry had looked at her like the man who thought Aunt Louise was wealthy and Louise would inherit a fortune, instead of nothing but a rundown old Edwardian house, full of furniture that nobody wanted.

When his expectations had been baulked he had cleared off very quickly, and now Louise knew what it was that Barry had seen in her. Money again. Her talent was a money-spinner. She was a plain girl, withdrawn, inhibited, but she was gifted at her job and naïve enough to hand over the takings because a good-looking man had told her he loved her.

She didn't have to ask, 'What have I got out of this?' because she had had Barry. He had taken her around, praised and flattered her, said that he loved her. He might even have married her, just as Douglas would have done if Aunt Louise *had* left her a fortune.

She said, 'You don't really love me, do you? I'm useful, that's all.'

'What's wrong with being useful?' He got up and came round to her. 'And of course I love you, but we're into a sticky patch and that money would be a godsend right now.' He lifted her up, into his arms, cajoling, 'Come on, sweetheart. Tell the woman you've got other business interests and you need the cash. Spin her a yarn.'

She shook her head. '*No.*' And after that it was ugly.

Barry lost his temper. He accused her of putting her career before his business, of being mean and mercenary, and finally of being a born spinster, a dried-up old maid.

He was off to Spain in the morning, he said. On his own. He would give her time to think things over, but if it was going to be this way he really couldn't see that they had much future together. If she wouldn't do this little thing for him.

Almost any other girl would have asked why her career should be considered less important than his, how she could possibly be mercenary when she had been handing over cash like peanuts for the past year, and laughed at the suggestion that she was dried up and sexless at twenty-two.

But all Louise could say was, 'Goodbye'. Then she walked out of the office, got into her car, and drove back to her flat.

Probably Barry believed that she would start negotiating to get that advance for him. He knew she hated arguments and strife, almost as much as she hated thunderstorms. They were her two phobias. She would do a great deal for the sake of peace and quiet, but he was mistaken if he thought she could be bullied. She didn't need time to think it over. She was through. She could never feel safe with Barry again.

She sat there for a little while with her silent tears, then she went into the bedroom and put her beach-wear and her new dresses back into drawers and wardrobe. When the cases were empty, and the drawers and wardrobe closed, she felt slightly better. There was no clutter now. Everywhere was in order and she was in control.

She went to the white telephone on the maple wood bureau and rang a number. She asked for Miss Cavell, and the woman who answered asked, 'Who's calling?'

'Louise Latham.'

'Oh, hello, Louise, it's Mary here.' Mary Edmunds was Paula's secretary. 'Paula's in America,' said Mary. 'Are there any problems?'

'No. Except—could I start on the house right away? I was taking a holiday first, as I told you, but it's fallen through and I don't feel like bothering to organise myself another. I'd rather get down to work.'

Louise had met Mary, who was very efficient and very likeable, when she first went along to view the house, take photographs and measurements, and get Miss Paula Cavell's instructions.

Later it was up to London for discussions with Miss Cavell, in Miss Cavell's penthouse apartment, and now all the designs had been passed, some of the materials were waiting, and Louise had been due to move into the house and start on its transformation in two weeks' time.

'Go ahead,' said Mary. 'The caretaker's up there. I'm following Paula myself tomorrow, but I'm sure she'll be delighted that you want to start ahead of schedule.'

Work was the one area of her life in which Louise was confident and successful. Work had never let her down. Her partnership with Barry was finished and she had learned another hard lesson. She was not going to be lucky in love, so she would do better to concentrate where she could expect a fair return.

This packing took her hardly any time. She filled the case with her working clothes, and the toilet accessories she would need. There were three or four months ahead of her, in Tir Glyn, the old manor house in the Welsh hills, and she welcomed the thought of solitude.

She had expected to be coming back here for weekends, or meeting Barry at halfway houses, but now all her plans had changed. It would be some time before she would feel like returning.

All her friends thought she was off on holiday with Barry, and she couldn't start explaining what had happened and why she wasn't. She rented an office over a paint-and-wallpaper shop in the town centre, but she had no staff. She would phone through to the shop when the two weeks were nearly up, and she should have been returning from Spain, and tell them where she was. They would send mail on for her, and go round to the flat occasionally. At one time she had worked in that shop, and the husband-and-wife who owned it had always been her best friends.

She was a good driver, fast but alert for hazards— perhaps because her parents had been killed in a road accident. It was a very long time ago, but her expertise at the wheel was above average and she knew exactly what her car could do, to the last fraction of acceleration.

She enjoyed driving. As her commissions increased she had been covering a wider area, but this was by far her biggest job yet, and the hardest to reach. The journey took her several hours, but she was more relaxed at the end of it than she had been when she started.

Tir Glyn was a beautiful house in a beautiful spot. She left the coast road, driving up a winding lane that rose steeply, overhung by trees and hedges of pink and white May, and in most places only one-vehicle wide.

There was a farmhouse on the lower slopes, but the lane only led to the house and the grounds of the house arriving, suddenly and unexpectedly, at huge wrought iron gates. They were open, the undergrowth grew up around them.

From the gates the drive was wide and sweeping, and everything looked lovely but neglected. The gardens were overgrown, the flight of shallow irregular steps, that led to a terrace surrounding the house, was moss-covered.

Most of the rooms inside were empty, the few pieces of furniture that remained were covered with dust sheets, but when the rooms were ready the beautiful carpets and curtains and furniture would arrive. It was an exciting challenge for Louise, and when she arrived here first, with Mary Edmunds, she hadn't been able to believe her eyes.

The whole thing was a tremendous stroke of luck. She had done some work in an hotel in the Lake District that had once been a stately home, and Paula Cavell had seen this and thought that perhaps Louise might be the interior decorator for the stately home that she had just acquired.

Paula's secretary had brought Louise down, and it had been like a dream come true for Louise. The rooms were all perfectly proportioned. As she walked through them she could see so clearly how they should look, and money was no object. Paula Cavell wanted the best of everything, and the cheque that Louise had already received, to meet the expense of materials, had been signed by James Fenton.

He was the industry magnate who was Miss Cavell's constant escort. This house was being prepared for him too. The study was very much a man's room, and the main bedroom had a man's dressing room leading off.

No one had actually said so, but Louise gathered from Mary that Paula and her millionaire—tall, dark and handsome, of course; Barry who had seen him confirmed that—would be getting married soon and this would be their home.

It was still a romantic thought, although Louise's own love life had gone sour. She loved the house, and she knew that it would make them a wonderful home.

Everything was very quiet when she arrived. There was no sign of life, and most of the windows had shutters drawn behind the glass panes. She sat in her van, which she would drive round to the back of the house in a minute or two, because that was where the stables-cum-garages were, and looked up at the old house, and told herself she would rather be here than in the villa in Spain.

Barry didn't love her. She was useful, and there was nothing wrong in being useful, but he didn't love her, and she was glad she had found out; and that, having found out, she hadn't had to hang around.

She would have no time here to mope. She was like the prince in *The Sleeping Beauty*, come to bring the castle back to life. Except that this wasn't a castle, it was a Victorian house, and she was no princess.

She was a great gawk of a girl, as her aunt had often told her, and Barry must have had no joy, pretending to love someone he found physically unappealing. He had been angry when he'd said that, but he had blurted out the truth, and Louise looked at her hands on the wheel and thought they were ugly.

She drove round and left her car in the yard at the back. There were no other cars to be seen, but the garage and stable doors were shut, so the caretaker's car might be garaged in there.

She knocked on the back door and waited. Nobody came and she knocked again, and when there was still no answer she tried the latch and the door opened.

She had presumed that Mary would have phoned through to warn the caretaker that Louise would be arriving, but perhaps Mary had thought Louise would do that herself. It didn't matter, the place wasn't locked up, somebody had to be on the premises somewhere.

She called 'Hello!' and her voice echoed so that it seemed that the house answered. No one else did, and her heels clattered along the flagstoned passage to the kitchen.

The kitchen was hopelessly out of date. Paula had been for having everything torn out and replaced by shining modern equipment, but she had finally agreed to a compromise. The modern equipment was coming, but chosen to blend with the comfortable old-fashioned look.

There was a kettle on the gas stove and crockery on the draining board by the sink, and Louise was suddenly longing for a cup of tea. She tried once more to make herself heard, shouting, 'Anybody home?' at the top of her voice from the kitchen door, then she filled the kettle and lit the gas and waited for the kettle to boil.

It was a lovely cup of tea, and she hoped that the caretaker wouldn't hurry back. What she would like best would be for no one else to be here. She could phone for provisions and cook her own meals. A little van delivered from a village about two miles down the road. When she was here last time, staying a couple of nights, one of the staff from Miss Cavell's London house had provided meals for Louise and Mary Edmunds.

There hadn't been a caretaker then and she wondered what the caretaker was like. She wasn't wanting company, and the house was big enough to avoid each other most of the time, but they would be under the same roof, so it would be better if the caretaker was congenial.

The tea was refreshing, and she ate an apple from a bag of apples on the dresser, then went out to her van and brought in her luggage. She supposed she would be in the same room she had had last time. It was near the top of the back staircase, a small room sparsely furnished with a single bed and a cupboard, bare floorboards, the walls faded to a patchy green.

She had it on her schedule for three walls in white, and one in a white paper patterned with small scarlet hearts, white skirting board and window frame, and a scarlet panelled door. It was going to make a pretty room, but it was near the end of the list, so she doubted if she would get much benefit from its face-lift.

The bed wasn't made up, there was only a mattress; she would have to get hold of that caretaker before she turned in. It wouldn't be for ages yet, it was only beginning to get dark, but she had had a longish journey and a trying day, and she wanted to make an early start in the morning.

She was starting upstairs, and she walked along the corridor to the main bedroom, empty except for ladders and boards. Shutters were over the windows in here, and she turned on a light while she worked the catch apart and folded them back.

The house needed airing, most of the rooms had been unused for goodness knows how long. When she tried to open the window it was a struggle, and she was just deciding to leave it till tomorrow when she saw the man below, coming towards the front of the house.

At that moment the stiff latch slipped back, and she pushed up the heavy window frame and leaned out. 'Hello there!' she called.

He stopped dead, staring up at her. He was in scruffy clothes and gumboots, a dark scruffy-looking man. 'Are you the caretaker?' she shouted.

'I am. Who the hell are you?'

So he hadn't been told to expect her. She began, 'I've come to start——' when he shouted,

'Get your neck in from under that window, the sash cords need replacing.'

That had been a silly risk to take, and she ducked back into the room and closed the window again.

He was waiting in the hall as she reached the main staircase. He turned on lights when she was half way down the stairs, and the sudden brilliance startled her so that she stood blinking for a moment. Then she said, 'What is this? Third degree?'

'You seem to have made yourself at home.'

She wasn't in a coat, just a tan jumper and camel skirt, and she was making herself at home because this was where she would be living for the next few months. She asked, 'Didn't Miss Edmunds tell you I was coming?'

'No.'

He was medium height, probably not much taller than she was, dark hair, eyebrows, eyes, skin tanned like a gipsy's, and needing a shave. He didn't move. He stood where he was and she reached the bottom of the stairs and stayed there, feeling that she would rather keep her distance. They were alone, and there was something slightly menacing about him.

She said, 'I'm here to do the interior decorating. I'm starting earlier than we planned.'

'Why?'

It wasn't really his business, she wasn't going to bother him, but of course she would rather be accepted than resented, and perhaps he couldn't help sounding surly.

'I was supposed to be going on a holiday,' she explained, 'but it fell through, so I phoned up and Miss Edmunds said it would be all right if I started work. That you were up here and it would be all right.' He was still looking grim and suspicious, although what else would she be doing here? She said, 'I'm sorry nobody let you know.'

'They could have phoned while I was out of the house.'

'Yes, that could have happened,' she agreed eagerly. 'I'm Louise Latham,' and after she had waited a few seconds she asked, 'What's your name?'

'Reading. Tom Reading.'

'And you're the caretaker?' It was a lonely job for anyone to take, and a short-term one. Where would he go from here? she wondered. And what did he do with himself while he was here? He was too old to be a student, who might use the peace to cram for an exam. He didn't look like a writer, or a recluse. It had to be a casual job and, apart from putting a roof over his head and a wage in his pocket, hardly rewarding and dead boring.

He said, as though he was answering her thoughts, 'I'm here to get the gardens back into shape, the care-taking's by the way.'

She was pleased about that. Of course the gardens would be restored too, but it was nice to know it was happening now. She would see them blossom and bloom while she worked on the house, and she smiled. 'And I'm here to make the house beautiful. I won't get in your way.'

He grinned back at her. The tan made his teeth look very white. 'As I'm out of doors most of the time, and you're in, there should be room for both of us. Which room are you having?'

'I've put my case into the one I had when I came here before. By the way, there's no bedding.'

'There are sheets and blankets in a chest.'

'Thank you.'

'You'll want an office, I suppose. And a sitting room. You can take your pick, but there's not much furni-ture.'

He wasn't sounding surly now, not welcoming, but she was here under instructions just as he was. She had a job to do for the people who were employing him. 'I know,' she said, 'I have been up here before.'

He reached her as she stood at the bottom of the stairs, and he was about four inches taller than she was. He looked tough, lean and sinewy, and he'd need to be to clear that garden. Beyond the house the trees had thickened into a wood.

He was weighing her up, she felt, and she found it hard to meet his eyes. 'I'm using the kitchen as a living room,' he said. 'There's a butler's pantry next to it, I'm sleeping in that for now. When everything's finished I don't know where they'll put me. Tell me before you start painting the pantry.'

Louise had fallen into step beside him, and he walked towards the kitchen. She said, 'I got myself a cup of tea and an apple, I hope you don't mind. I didn't stop to think about bringing any food.'

'There's food.'

She had known there would be someone else up here and she was glad it was a gardener, because he would be creating the setting for her house. 'What are you doing with the gardens?' she asked. 'What will they look like?'

'You'd better get your room to rights. The linen chest's on the landing under the oriel window.' She thought she was being snubbed, but he went on, 'I need a wash and then you're welcome to a meal if you want it. I'll tell you the plans for the garden and you can tell me what you're going to do with the house.'

'Are you interested in the house?'

'I'm probably going to live in it.' He sat down and took off his gumboots, revealing bare feet. 'In the servants' quarters, of course. Are they on your list?'

'Yes.'

'They'd better be.'

She found herself smiling, joking, 'Tell me which is going to be your room and maybe——'

'Oh, I take what I'm given.'

She laughed at that, 'Hmmm?' and was surprised at herself. The man was a stranger. She must be careful what she said and how she acted, she didn't want too much familiarity.

He took off a brown lightweight anorak and hung it on a hook behind the door. It had a tear in the sleeve and she thought—his wife will have to darn that for him. If he has a wife surely she's here.

'I could do with a wash myself,' she said. 'I'll be back in about fifteen minutes, if that's all right.'

She found the bedding chest and made up her bed. She should sleep peacefully here. There would be no sounds of traffic or other people's lives, as there were in her apartment, no letters, no phone ringing for her.

She didn't imagine that Barry would try to get in touch with her today, but by tomorrow he would be expecting her to contact him, apologising, wanting to make it up again, promising to try to get that advance.

But he was wrong. She wasn't that infatuated. She didn't want arms around her that meant nothing at all.

She went to the nearest bathroom to her bedroom, and washed away the grime of the journey. In the old mahogany-framed mirror, fixed to the wall, she touched up her lips with a coral lipstick and smoothed brown shadow on her lids, tipping her lashes with brown mascara. Her eyes were hazel, and she had the pale skin that comes with pale fine hair—in her case a light reddish brown—and can look either devastating or dreary.

Louise felt that she must have been born looking washed out. Until she put colour on her face she was colourless, and even when she was in full make-up no one was ever going to say, 'There goes a girl with zing!'

They said it about some of the rooms she produced. She could put pep into a teenager's bedsitter, just as she could create beautiful rooms, romantic rooms, exciting and trendy rooms.

She was a dreamer, an artist, and a feverishly hard-working professional, but she couldn't make herself into a beauty. One day, she thought, if she became a real success earning really big money, she would spend it all on herself and maybe that would do the trick, and give her the confidence that had been knocked out of her again today.

She had thought that Barry loved her. It had often seemed too good to be true, but they had been going to get engaged, and perhaps it was as well she had company this evening. She could talk shop with Tom Reading, about the house and the garden, and keep reminding herself how lucky she had been to get this commission.

He was in the kitchen, when she went downstairs, putting food on the table from the fridge. He was still wearing the dark plaid open-necked shirt, but he had shaved and without the stubble of beard and moustache he should have looked smoother, less of a scrapper. But he didn't.

Louise sat down and looked at him and thought—he's ugly. And then—no, he isn't. It was an interesting face: the nose strong and straight, the mouth thin, tight-lipped until he grinned at her. 'Recognise me?'

'Should I?' She had been staring harder than was polite, and she shook her head. 'I don't think we've ever met.'

'I know we haven't,' he said. 'I'd have remembered. Help yourself.'

There were two plates, two cups and saucers, and a haphazard collection of cheese, pork pie, jars of pickles, sliced loaf and a slab of butter still in its wrapping paper. She said impulsively, 'Just the two of us? I mean, there's no one else here?'

'Did you expect anyone else? M'lady isn't in residence yet. We're the advance guard.'

The way he said 'M'lady' sounded ironic, although Paula's exquisite looks must impress any man. She could be as out of reach as the stars for Tom Reading, but who knew how Paula's tastes ran? And Louise, embarrassed at the way her thoughts were running, hastily reached for the bread and butter.

Perhaps she looked embarrassed, because he said, 'You don't need to worry about there being only the two of us.'

Of course she wasn't worried. She knew that this man wouldn't make a nuisance of himself. There was too much self-control in the straight hard line of that mouth.

'I'm not worried,' she stammered, 'I just wondered if your wife was here or——'

'I'd be very surprised if she was,' he said laconically. 'I don't have one.'

'Oh!' Now it sounded as if she was curious about his marital status, the kind of girl whose first question to any man under the age of seventy is 'Are you married?' and she took a deep breath, trying to get things straight. 'It doesn't bother me if I'm up here with one man or fifty. The only thing I'm bothered about is doing the job they'll be paying me for.'

He grinned. 'Now fifty might be a different matter. There'd be real safety in numbers with fifty,' and again she found herself laughing with him. 'But I've got a wood to cut down, so I'm not going to have much energy left over, you're not going to have any trouble with me,' he said.

That was something she sensed in him—energy. He was sitting at the table now, opposite her, relaxed, pouring out a cup of tea which was hardly a dynamic occupation. But she got the impression that he was almost tireless, that there was a tremendous fund of vitality in him.

She asked, 'You're not really going to cut down all the trees, are you?' and he said as though the idea appalled him,

'Good God, no, I don't cut down trees unless there's a very good reason. I'm just clearing a way through them. The garden isn't being changed, it's all right as it is. It only needs taming.'

'Taming?' she echoed.

'We've got to give the flowers a chance.' He spooned sugar into his cup and pushed the teapot over to her. 'The trees and the grasses are strangling them.'

'It sounds like a jungle out there.'

'Like life.'

He could say that again. She was glad she was here, and away from life for a while. She said contentedly, 'All I've got to do to plant my flowers is get the old paint and paper off the walls.'

When he smiled at her he looked younger, almost carefree. 'And I'll hold back the jungle outside. We've got a partnership going here.'

It was odd he should say that. This morning she had had a partnership with Barry, now for a while she was linked with a very different kind of man. Well, there would be something to show at the end of this partnership, a beautiful house in a beautiful garden, which could be the take-off springboard for her career.

'I'd like that,' she said.

CHAPTER TWO

'WHAT are you starting on?' Tom Reading asked her, and Louise put down the knife with which she had been cutting up her pork pie, as though she needed both hands and all her concentration to explain what she would be doing in this house.

'The main bedroom. My instructions are to do that and the drawing room first. I'll be getting the old paint and paper off the bedroom tomorrow.'

'Sounds a dirty job.'

She agreed, happily.

'You do it all yourself?'

'Yes.'

'I'd have thought as a designer you'd have employed someone else to get the place ready.'

'I might some time, but I quite enjoy it. And this is the biggest job I've ever had.' She wasn't going to admit that to everybody. Perhaps she shouldn't have mentioned it at all, because he was looking at her rather doubtfully.

'You think you'll manage it?'

'Of course,' she said airily. She'd manage if it killed her, and it would do nothing of the sort. It would set her up in body and mind, and with any luck in business.

'You don't look very strong to me.' He had heavy brows that came down in a straight line when he frowned, and his dark eyes were piercing. He looked the kind of man who'd see straight through you. 'Are you?' he demanded.

'Oh yes.' Not that he need worry if she was delicate as a flower or strong as a horse. 'You keep the jungle back,' she said, 'and I'll make this into a lovely house.'

She looked around the kitchen, smiling, seeing it as it was going to be, and beyond the kitchen door the whole house. She could feel him watching her and he was part of her dream, the man who was here to make a beautiful garden. When he asked, 'How long have you been an interior decorator?' she said lightly,

'Oh, about twenty years.'

'*What?*'

'It started with a dolls' house.'

... The only toy that had gone with her to Aunt Louise's, as a child of four, both mother and father dead. To Aunt Louise, who was obsessed with gentility. Louise was taken into that house because of what the neighbours might say if Miss Manderley's only niece had been allowed to go into a home or to foster-parents. The dolls' house had been Louise's secret dream world, a house where people were happy, and over the years, colouring and painting minutely patterned wallpapers, she had made new rooms of old. When Aunt Louise sent it to a jumble sale Louise told herself that she had outgrown it. But she missed it, and the family of pipe-cleaner dolls, as though she had lost a living family and a home ...

'Start small,' said Tom Reading. 'What did you go on to from there?'

He didn't seem like a man who would ask about anything unless he genuinely wanted his questions answered. So she told him, 'I started work in a wall-paper shop when I left school. They had little alcoves all round to show off the papers, with bits of furniture here and there, and I used to help do those. Then, when customers were choosing, I found that I could often help them. I used to put people into settings in my mind.'

She smiled, 'I still do that, all the time. I look at strangers and put them into living rooms. Or bedrooms.' He raised a quizzical eyebrow, but she didn't feel embarrassed, only amused.

'It's a strictly professional exercise,' she said cheerfully. 'They're just standing there, fully clad, even if I'm designing a bathroom around them.'

'Where would you put me?' He looked comfortable where he was, sitting on an old chair at an old table, in this big old kitchen, as though this was his kind of setting.

Or was it? She couldn't quite work him out, but she played along. 'How about a log cabin in the Rockies? You look like a hunting man.'

'Wrong,' he said, 'I'm not. So you started to advise the customers?'

'Yes.' When she had answered all his questions she would ask a few. 'And the shop I worked in does a professional service, as well as selling D.I.Y. materials, and Barbara, Mrs Cole—she and her husband own the shop—suggested that I went along and looked at some of the rooms if people wanted advice.'

Louise paused, and he waited, so she went on, 'And I went, and I helped the men who were doing the work. And that was my apprenticeship. That was how I learned my job.'

'And now you're beginning to make a name for yourself?'

She was beginning to be recommended. She said, 'I'm hoping Tir Glyn is going to do that for me. I was very lucky to get this commission.'

'Were you?'

'Oh yes.' She went back to eating her pie. After a couple of mouthfuls she said, 'I've always been lucky in work.'

... But not in love. Douglas had thought that Aunt Louise was wealthy and that Louise was an heiress. When the will was read, and all that Miss Louise

Mannering had had to bequeath turned out to be a shabby-genteel house, Douglas had cooled off as rapidly as though he had stepped into freezing water.

While she was alive Aunt Louise had refused to have anything changed in the house. Woodwork was kept as dark oak. Walls stayed in sombre shades. It could have gone on the market as a solid property, but it was nobody's dream house until Louise went through it, bringing colour and light.

Aunt Louise probably turned in her grave, but when the house was eventually sold Louise got almost twice the first suggested price. By then she had worked Douglas right out of her system, and she decided to set up in business on her own, moving into a flat, renting an office from Barbara and Alan Cole.

She was free of Douglas, but Barry's firm had done some structural alterations on the house for her, and she was soon involved with Barry. She had invested most of her money from the house sale with him. She had handed over to Barry, and now she had to work him out of her system too. She had been twice bitten, but this time she *had* learned her lesson ...

'Only in work?' said Tom Reading, and she grimaced instinctively, because she had given herself away there. She had no intention of going into details, but it would have been stupid to pretend she didn't understand what he meant. The only thing she could do was smile and say something flippant that might change the subject. Like, 'We can't all be Paula Cavells. Famous *and* marrying a millionaire.'

'Is she marrying a millionaire?'

She said hastily, 'I don't know.' Mary Edmunds hadn't exactly said so, but she had certainly given Louise that impression. 'But there is James Fenton in the background, isn't there, and this is hardly a bachelor girl pad, is it?'

Tom grinned. 'Depends on the bachelor girl. She could get fifty men in here.'

Louise's lips twitched. James Fenton had signed the cheque she had received, so he must have an interest in the place. She said, 'I shouldn't think he's expecting her to be entertaining another forty-nine admirers.'

This was fairly scandalous nonsense, but it was better to laugh than cry. If she had been here alone she might have been crying.

Tom was chuckling, presumably at the thought of the selective Miss Cavell with a male harem, and Louise asked, 'Have you met him?'

'Fenton? Yes. But he didn't have much to say to me, she gave the orders.'

'She did with me too.' Paula Cavell had been everything in the flesh that her television image promised, so far as appearances went, but Louise had met a lot of people she had liked more. Paula didn't bother with good manners for hired helps, and when Louise had asked Mary Edmunds later how she got on with Paula Mary had admitted that Miss Cavell was not easy to work for.

Louise wouldn't have wanted Mary Edmunds' job, nor, she supposed, Tom Reading's. She wondered how Paula had given her orders to him, because no matter how good the wages she couldn't imagine him kowtowing.

She asked him, 'How did you get this job? Are you local?' He was dark, taut-muscled, not over-tall. He could be Celtic.

'I was working a few miles from here. The old chap who did these gardens gave up before the house was sold. He was into his seventies.' That was why they were so neglected. Even a man who was strong and young would be hard put to control this jungle single-handed. 'When the place was bought I came along,' said Tom, 'and a bloke called Gillian took me on.'

'Who's he?' Louise hadn't heard that name.

'The agent who was getting the staff together.' Of course they'd need a staff here, Tir Glyn was a big house. After Louise left the people whose home it was going to be would move in, to live their lives here. 'He'll be around,' said Tom. 'You'll be meeting him.'

She wasn't very interested in Mr Gillian. He hadn't hired her. She asked, 'Have you always been a gardener?'

'My father was. I've done other things in my time.'

Again she felt that prickle of nerves. What other things? she wondered, and it was an obvious question, but she didn't ask right away, and before she could speak he said, 'Do you have a family?'

'No. Do you?'

'No.'

Two lonely people, although not having a family didn't mean you had to be lonely. You could have friends, you could be self-sufficient. She had friends. He probably did too, and he looked as though he could take very good care of himself, which didn't detract from his attraction. The gardens might be a challenge now, like the house was. When they were tamed she wondered if he would still find fulfilment here. 'Will you stay on here?' she asked.

'For a while.' So he was one of those who moved on.

'If I had a place like this to work in,' she said, 'I'd say,' and he smiled,

'Would you? Where do you live? What kind of home have you made for yourself?'

'Not a home really,' she had to admit. 'Just an apartment.' She had designed it for her working image, but one day she would have a permanent home that she would plan with love. Of course it would be nowhere like as grand as this place, but it was waiting for her.

'One day,' she said.

She slept soundly that night. When she woke she remembered yesterday, and that she should have been flying to the sun with Barry today. But the sun was shining here too, early morning sunshine was streaming in through the window, and she felt much less depressed than she had expected to feel.

Hardly depressed at all. Eager to get up and start the day. She sat up in bed, hands clasped around her ankles, chin on her knees, and surveyed the dingy room. 'Your time will come, my beauty,' she told it. 'Just have a little patience.'

Then she burst out laughing, because she could have been saying that to herself.

She dressed in jeans and shirt and flat pumps, and took the old blue scarf that she would be using to tie up her hair, and went downstairs. The smell of frying bacon reached her as she tapped on the kitchen door. 'Come in!' Tom called. He was dressed like yesterday, sitting at the table drinking coffee.

'Good morning,' she said. 'Will it be all right if I get myself some breakfast?'

'It's waiting for you.' There was bacon in the pan, and an uncooked egg and tomato on a plate, and the sun was shining in here too.

'Thank you,' she said.

'Sausages do you for dinner?' he asked.

He was taking it for granted that they would be eating together and it would have been ridiculous for her to take her food off on a tray into another room. Unless they began to get on each other's nerves.

'Anything will do for me,' she said, cooking her breakfast. He poured a second cup of coffee and she drank some. 'Marvellous!' she said rapturously. 'Sun shining and coming down to coffee all ready.'

He leaned back in his chair, smiling at her, and she wondered if she had sounded gushing. But she had been so thankful to wake up feeling cheerful, and so surprised.

'Where were you going, on this holiday you didn't go on?' he asked.

'Spain.'

'Why didn't you go?'

She brought her breakfast to the table, and took another sip of coffee. Then she said flatly, 'I had a row with a man,' and he grinned.

'That's the worst of being a natural redhead.' But there was no fire in her. All she had said was goodbye. 'We could always have a bottle of Spanish wine with the sausages to make you feel you're not missing too much,' he suggested, and she almost frowned, suspecting that he was laughing at her. Then she laughed instead.

'Now where would we get Spanish wine up here?'

'There's a phone.'

'You're not suggesting we ring the nearest off-licence and ask them to deliver?'

'No? Well, I've always got the bike.'

'If you're going shopping on it,' she said, 'I'll stick to Spanish orange juice.'

'There's a tin of that in the fridge.'

'It *is* as good as being on holiday,' she smiled.

'Except you won't get much of a suntan. Unless you come out and help me cut the grass.'

'Not likely!' she said cheerfully.

He had already eaten his breakfast. He went off to start scything the front lawns, and Louise was hungry, and as she ate her breakfast she realised that she had meant what she had just said. She was going to enjoy

being here as much as she would have enjoyed those
two weeks in the villa in Denia.

She wasn't going to pine for Barry. Maybe she had
spirit after all, and for the first time she was a free
spirit. She would show him, and everybody, what she
could do.

She decided to use the dining room for her papers.
There was a big table in there, long enough to seat a
dozen, and with massively ugly carved legs. It wasn't
staying. The dining room was going elegantly Regency,
with a genuine oval Regency table and matching chairs
arriving. Dinners would be smaller and more intimate,
but the Victorian table was ideal for Louise's sketches
and plans.

She could spread everything out, where she could see
it at a glance. She opened the shutters, so that light
came into the room, and put her portfolio and briefcase on the table.

Then she went upstairs to the main bedroom. In
here wallpaper had faded, and paint had darkened,
through the years, but the last time it had been decor-
ated it had been a thoroughly professional job. There
was only one layer of paper and the paint was smooth
on the wood. She wouldn't be stripping down through
messy layers of old patterns and colour schemes.

She wedged the window open with a piece of wood,
and she could see Tom below, cutting the grass on
what was going to be a large lawn in front of the
house. He was stripped to the waist, his back as darkly
tanned as his face. Those other jobs of his must have
been open-air work.

He hasn't been down the mines or in prison, she
thought, smiling at that thought. At least she hoped it
was funny, the bit about him not having been in
prison.

She began to steam-strip the walls, and the paper

came off in long satisfying rolls. The plaster behind was sound, which was all to the good. She might even have this room prepared by the end of the day. Tins of paint and rolls of paper were downstairs in the draw-ing room, and her fingers were itching to finish the preparations and start the beautifying.

She sang to herself as she worked, softly because she would have felt a fool if her voice had floated down over the gardens. From time to time she glanced out, and once he saw her and waved and she almost jumped back as though she had been caught spying. But she waved back instead.

Some time, of course, she would have to take on someone to help her, if her commissions increased as she hoped they would. But she enjoyed working alone, in her own way. Now she had the best of both worlds, someone working with her but doing their own thing. Tonight she would walk round the gardens and see what progress he had made. Although he must have had a few weeks' start on her.

The ringing of the telephone brought her down-stairs into the hall. There was a phone in the study, and she was hurrying to answer it when she suddenly realised that this could be Barry.

By now he would be almost ready to set off for the airport. By now he would have expected her to ring him. He might have gone to her apartment and found that she wasn't there. Someone might have told him she'd gone yesterday afternoon, and he could have worked out that she might have come here.

The phone went on ringing. Whoever it was was persistent, and she opened the front door so that the ringing floated over the still air. 'The phone!' she called.

Tom came through the grass, across the flagstoned forecourt, and up the steps. 'Something in your contract against you answering telephones?' he inquired, and she bit her lip, feeling herself beginning to flush, stammering,

'It could be for me. If it is—if it's a man called Barry Mason—I don't want him to know I'm here.'

He shrugged and went into the study. The ringing. stopped and he returned almost at once. He said, 'It was to tell me you're on your way.'

She relaxed and smiled unsteadily. She had made an unnecessary fuss, and he was expecting an explanation. 'Is Mason the man you should have gone to Spain with?' he asked.

'Yes.'

'And he doesn't know you're here?'

'No.' Well, she hoped he didn't. 'Unless he's spoken to Miss Cavell's secretary and asked her, but I think he'd be more likely to ring here first.' She paused for a moment, and then she said, 'No, I don't. I think he'd be more likely to go to Spain.'

'The man's a fool,' said Tom, and that made her smile.

'I'm glad you think so,' she said.

'How's it going?' He jerked his head, indicating the room upstairs.

'Fine. How about a cup of coffee?' It was nearly eleven o'clock, and if he didn't break for elevenses she did.

'Good idea,' he said.

She brought two cups out and Tom was standing by the low stone wall of the terrace. There was an ornate wrought iron bench a little way along, she had thought they might sit on that, but she joined him where he was, and looked down the sweep of the hill to the valley, and across to other hills rising. There was a village down there, and a road, but the green hills dwarfed everything.

It was very quiet, just the faint hum of insects, and a twittering among the birds in the trees behind the house, and she said huskily, 'It's a wonderful view. They couldn't have found a more peaceful place.'

He nodded, he agreed with her, and they stood together, saying nothing, drinking their coffee and letting the peace wash over them. At least that was what Louise did. Tom might have been thinking about his work, or about anything, but she didn't think. She gave herself up to the sensation of peace, breathing deeply, clean air with the scent of newly cut grass.

When her cup was drained she was ready to go back to work and she held out a hand for his empty cup and smiled. 'Do you eat lunch?' she asked.

'Bread and cheese, I have it where I'm working. I get a meal about six.'

She would have done a good day's stint before six o'clock and she would get the evening meal ready. 'I'll see you at six, then,' she said.

She worked hard, until the walls in the big bedroom were bare and the paintwork was ready for the undercoat. She started on the dressing room, leading off, and she was scraping the treated skirting board, down on her knees, when a shadow fell across her.

'Are you working through the night?' Tom asked.

Louise sat back on her heels, surprised that she hadn't heard him coming. She must have been really concentrating, and she had had her head down, and gumboots on a wooden floor don't make much noise. It was twenty minutes to seven, she hadn't glanced at her watch in ages, and she said, 'Drat, I'd meant to cook the sausages.'

'They're nearly ready. Are you?'

'Yes.' She had a moment's stiffness trying to rise, and he helped her to her feet. 'Thanks, I got a bit cramped down there.' She pulled off her headscarf, shaking her

hair loose, then flexed her shoulders back, to counter-
act the hunching over the skirting board, wincing.

'Ten minutes,' said Tom, and when he had gone she
thought that he had lifted her gently and easily, with
no fuss. She put her equipment tidily by, and hurried
to wash in the old-fashioned bathroom, feeling warm,
comforted somehow. As though something surprising
and nice had happened to her.

It was a beautiful evening. In the kitchen Tom had
food on a tray and he said, 'We'll eat outside, on the
terrace.'

He wouldn't be able to do that when the house was
full, but for a while he had the run of the place, and so
did Louise. Dining on the terrace sounded very graci-
ous living, even if they were dining on sausages.

He had put a table in front of the wrought iron
bench and he put the tray on that, and Louise seated
herself, with the panoramic view spread out in front of
her again, but this time there was a sunset too. The
sun had slipped down behind the hills in a glorious
scarlet sky. Red sky at night, tomorrow would be as
beautiful as today.

The smell of cut grass was still in the air, and there
was an evening hush over everything. They ate without talking much. Louise felt that it would be sacri-
lege to disturb the peace, and she always had been a
quiet girl, too reserved perhaps, too inhibited.

The meal was almost finished when Tom smiled at
her. She had been looking into the distance and she
sighed, bemused with pleasure, and he suddenly
smiled at her.

'There can't be anywhere more beautiful than this
in the whole world,' she said, and she was glad there
was someone sharing it with her. 'Not that I've been
far to make comparisons,' she said. 'Have you?'

'I worked in Canada for a while.' So maybe she
wasn't so much off the mark in putting him in a cabin
in the Rockies, but he didn't volunteer any more in-
formation and after a while she said,

'I'd like to travel. I've had a couple of holidays, to
Spain and Italy, in the past two years, but I'd like to
go to all sorts of places.'

'When you're famous and rich?'

'Then there's a lot of hard work ahead of me first.'
She had been finishing her meal with an apple. She
put the core on the plate. 'I think I'm going for a
walk,' she said, and asked him, 'will you come with
me?'

It was a natural invitation. It was lonely up here,
and night would be falling before too long, and she
didn't know the paths. But usually she liked walking
alone, and she wouldn't be likely to lose sight of the
house, and she was surprised to realise how much she
wanted Tom with her, while she discovered the gardens and grounds around 'her' house.

'I'll show you round the gardens,' he said.

Louise walked carefully down the steps with their
patches of moss. She would have thought he would
have cleared those, they were surely dangerous. 'How
long have you been here?' she asked.

'A couple of days.'

'Oh. I thought you'd been here longer.'

'Does it look as though I have?'

They were walking over the lawn he had been scything. The grass was shorter but ragged. Bushes and
hedges were high and unkempt, and flowers and weeds
grew together.

'Not here, no,' she agreed, 'but I thought you'd been
working in the wood, and isn't there a kitchen garden?'

He nodded, there was a kitchen garden. 'I was taken

on about six weeks ago,' he said, 'but I couldn't get here right away.'

'Oh,' she said again. She had never been a country girl. Aunt Louise's garden had been a rigid lawn, front of the house and back, edged by shrubs, kept under strict control by a gardener who came for a couple of hours each week and was as unlike Tom as this garden was unlike Aunt Louise's garden.

This garden was without any order. It had been left to grow as it chose for a long time, a year or more. Roses, from deepest red to pure white, bloomed among the yellow gorse and broom. Wild flowers and cultivated flowers mingled, overgrown by grass and groundsel and purple vetch. There were marigolds and daisies, foxgloves and celandines, cut back from the paths but flourishing riotously, and Louise sighed, 'They're so pretty, it will be a shame to pull them up.'

He smiled. 'Don't you approve of a tidy garden? Everything in its place. Isn't that how you design your rooms?'

Yes, it was. She laughed. 'I haven't done many wild rooms. Wild rooms just happen. People who live in them don't need anyone else to tell them what their favourite colour is.'

Her laughter seemed loud, although it wasn't. It was because there were no other sounds. 'What's your favourite colour?' asked Tom.

'All of them.' She loved colour, that was why she resented her own colourless skin and personality. Although up here she didn't feel so colourless. Perhaps it was because of the house, where she would be using colour to make the rooms vibrant and alive. And there was something about the gardens, under the flaming sunset, that got beneath her skin, sharpening her senses.

Then there was Tom, keeping her guessing and

wondering. Douglas and Barry hadn't really surprised her. She had been disillusioned by them but not surprised. In both cases she had slipped into a relationship that seemed to promise a peaceful loving. In both cases the price had been too high, and strictly cash. But she couldn't recall walking beside either man with this feeling of heightened anticipation. If the house and gardens had been her own she could hardly have been enjoying her stroll around the grounds more.

He was telling her the plans for the garden's layout, and soon she would tell him what she was going to do with the house.

The garden was not being changed too drastically. Round the side of the house was a walled and sheltered half-acre, which had produced fruit and vegetables and would do again; and behind the house, beyond the yard and the outbuildings, were the trees.

Dusk was falling as they slowly skirted the house, coming back to the front lawns and the drive down to the old wrought-iron gates. When the gates were repaired and repainted, and swinging free from the undergrowth again, this would be a spectacular entrance.

'Isn't she having a swimming pool?' Louise was half joking. It would be chilly up here in the winter, but Paula Cavell might well fancy a pool for the hot summer days. Or have one enclosed and heated.

'If she is she hasn't asked me to dig it,' said Tom. 'But she wants that front lawn so that a helicopter can land on it.'

Louise whistled soundlessly at how the other half lived. 'Imagine sailing up here in a helicopter! That would beat your bike, or my old van.'

He smiled. She had said it to make him smile. When he smiled he did look younger. They were going to get on together, and that was lucky as they were stuck up here together. It could have been an awkward situation, but it wasn't. Not at all.

Nothing more was said about Louise choosing a sitting room for herself. They spent the evening in the kitchen. She described the house for him, room by room, while he took a lawn-mower engine to pieces on the kitchen table, on several large sheets of newspaper.

She did most of the talking, because he wanted to know about the house. She couldn't have talked about herself nearly so fluently. She sat there, with shining eyes, describing how the panelling in the hall and the balustrade of the staircase would glow when she had cleaned off the dulling grime, and how the colour—half way between peach and parchment—of upper walls and ceiling would carry through into the drawing room to take on the sheen of silk.

When he asked, 'How will you feel about leaving here when you've finished?' she admitted,

'I don't know; I could hate going. The last old house I did was the one Aunt Louise left me two years ago, and of course that was nothing compared with here.'

He looked at her inquiringly, asking about Aunt Louise without speaking, and she said slowly, 'My aunt reared me. My parents were killed in a car crash when I was a baby.'

'Were you happy with her?'

Louise licked her dry lips. She didn't like talking about herself. She didn't do it, but he was waiting for an answer, and somehow she couldn't say, 'Of course.' 'No,' she said.

'Why not?'

'She wasn't a lovable woman.' She didn't want to talk about Aunt Louise either. 'Where were you born?' she asked shortly. 'Were you happy as a child? What other trades have you had, besides gardening?

In Canada—what were you doing in Canada?'

He put down the spring he had been dowsing in a tin of some sort of cleanser, and a damp ring slowly spread out around it on the newspaper. 'Sorry,' he said, 'I don't usually ask so many questions.'

'It doesn't matter,' she said stiffly.

She could feel the stiffness in her spine. She was sitting so upright that she must look like Aunt Louise used to look, and it was silly to get so tense because she had been asked a couple of personal things.

She could always have said that she had had a happy childhood, and she need never have mentioned Aunt Louise in the first place.

She stood up. 'I think it's time I went to bed. There's a lot of work to do tomorrow. I'm sorry I was touchy.'

Tom smiled, and she suddenly wanted to sit down again and say, 'You can ask me all the questions you want. I'm not very interesting, but I think I'm glad you're interested in me.'

She didn't do that, but they both laughed a little, as though a misunderstanding had been cleared up. Then she went off up the back stairs, with the same comforted feeling she had had when he'd helped her to her feet earlier this evening, as though she was close to someone strong and caring.

CHAPTER THREE

LOUISE was having an idyllic time. She couldn't remember any time when she had enjoyed herself more than in this glorious empty house. Although the preparations were hard work, leaving her dirty and sticky

and tired, after the preparations she was making it all
beautiful.

She finished the main bedroom that first week, in a
green/blue/gold scheme. A magnificent canopied bed
was coming in here, and rich gold and green fabrics for
windows and bed drapes. The dressing room, leading
off, was plain by comparison. In there walls were a
subtle matt green, and the furniture would be fitted.

'Hope you'll approve, Mr Fenton,' she said, as she
stepped back from the dressing room, and she went to
find Tom to ask for his approval too.

He was digging in the kitchen garden. The ground
was hard and he welcomed the break. He hadn't been
upstairs since she began the decorating, Louise wanted
a room finished before he saw, and he was suitably
impressed. '*Very* nice,' he said, looking around.

'This is the star's room, of course, so it's the biggest
and the grandest. I'm looking forward to doing some
of the smaller bedrooms, the one next door is going to
be full of blue roses. Do you think he'll like his dressing room?'

Tom put his head through the dressing-room door.
'It's what they ordered, isn't it?'

'Oh yes.'

'If he doesn't like it he damn well ought to.'

'That's right, and the same goes for the garden.'
They smiled at each other, working partners, and he
helped her carry the ladders and boards downstairs, so
that she could start from scratch, all over again, in the
drawing room.

She was getting used now to this big empty house,
walking around it and never feeling lonely. That was
probably because Tom was usually in earshot. He was
outside most of the time, but if she had opened a
window and shouted her voice would have reached
him. She never had done. If she needed to speak to

him about anything she went and looked for him. She could never remember shouting at the top of her voice in her whole life.

Tom was a reassuring man to have around, completely capable. She had nothing to do but her work, the running of the house was his business. He was often on the phone in the study about things, but she never used the phone, she was strictly incommunicado up here.

He phoned down to the village store and ordered the provisions to be delivered, and sometimes she prepared the evening meal and sometimes he did. It was never anything fancy, easily cooked food or cold, which they ate on the verandah, because every evening was warm.

Louise was at ease with Tom. She hoped they would stay friends after she had left here. They talked together, like old friends, and sometimes discussed the future vaguely. Louise would go where her work took her, and so would he, although he reckoned this place would need him for a while.

It would need Louise for about four months, and that seemed a long, long time. She didn't really want to think beyond that. She was contented. She would have been happy to stay up here for ever, working in the beautiful rooms, coming out into the fresh air and the sunshine, eating her meals with Tom, talking and walking with him, sleeping soundly at night.

When the first week was over he asked her, 'Shan't you be going home for the weekend?'

It was breakfast on Saturday. She was making toast and he was waiting for a slice. She said, 'I'm not going anywhere until I've finished the house.'

'You're not?' That staggered him. 'You're holing up here for how long?'

'As long as it takes me,' she said, removing the

popped-up toast and handing it over to him by the butter dish.

'That's single-minded.' He sounded as though she was overdoing devotion to duty. 'Have you brought all you'll need for a good long stay?'

'I can drive out and buy more clothes and things, of course, but I'm living here until Tir Glyn's ready for Miss Cavell to move in.' Some furniture for the main bedroom and the drawing room were due to arrive first, that meant that Paula could be paying flying visits, but she was anxious for the house to be completed, and Mary had hinted that fixing the wedding date had something to do with that.

'Why not?' Louise demanded. 'You live in on the job, don't you? You don't take a weekend off to go home.'

'Oh yes, I do,' said Tom promptly.

She had been buttering the toast herself. 'Go home?' she said, starting on the second round.

'Take a weekend off.'

'Yes, of course.' She sat down with her round of toast, and reached for the marmalade jar, asking casually, 'Will you be away this weekend?'

'No.'

She was glad about that, it might have been lonely on her own. She wondered where he went and who he met. He must have friends, although he didn't talk about them. She still didn't know much about him, and it wasn't until today, later, during the morning, that she asked him, 'Were you ever married?'

They were drinking coffee, around eleven o'clock, sitting on the steps leading down from the terrace, and Louise had been talking about Barbara and Alan Cole, who were such good friends. It had been their fifteenth wedding anniversary a couple of days before she came here, they had had a party. She had been telling Tom about the party, then she asked him, 'Were you ever married?'

'No.' He sounded cheerful, not as though anyone had broken his heart on the way. 'And neither were you,' he said.

'How do you know?' She darted a quick wary look. Barry had said she was a dried-up old maid, perhaps it showed.

'You haven't had the time,' said Tom. 'All your energies have gone into your career. How old are you, anyway? Twenty?'

'Twenty-two,' and she had thought she looked older. 'You've had time,' she said mischievously. Right now she didn't feel any older than twenty, it was nice to hear she didn't look it.

He grinned, and she asked, 'How old are you?'

'Ten years older than you. You'll be married long before you're my age.'

She felt so comfortable with Tom. She held her mug of coffee in her cupped hands, and thought that the moss on the steps wasn't a bad idea. It made them softer to sit on, if you didn't mind the seat of your jeans turning green. 'You don't think I'm a born spinster?' she asked.

Tom eyed her consideringly, then he said, 'I wouldn't have thought so. Are you?' He sounded as though it would be her own choice, and that was cheering.

'Barry said I was,' she said.

His eyebrows joined. 'Who? Ah yes,' he remembered. 'During that row before you didn't go to Spain?' She nodded. 'Was it meant to be an insult?'

She nodded again, and Tom shrugged and finished his coffee. 'Forget it,' he advised. 'You can't afford to be too sensitive in this world.'

He wouldn't let snide remarks fester under his skin.

He'd shrug them off, or more likely come back with something that would hit harder and last longer, which Louise had never been able to do. All she could say to Barry was, 'Goodbye.'

'It doesn't do to worry about what other people think about you, does it?' she said.

'Ninety-nine times out of a hundred, no,' said Tom.

Louise put down her mug, still about a third full, on an uneven patch of moss on the step beside her, and as it tippled over and spilt she smiled ruefully. 'But every time I do anything like that, or bump into anything, I can still hear Aunt Louise calling me a great gawk of a girl.'

'A *what*?'

She repeated, 'A great gawk,' and Tom chuckled.

'I thought you said a great auk.' The giggles came at that, her shoulders were shaking as he went on, 'But that bird's extinct, and you're a very much alive bird.' She felt very much alive. 'And why a gawk?' he asked.

'Because I was. I was always longer and skinnier than I ought to be.' She still was, but now her long legs in jeans didn't displease her, although the flat shapeless comfortable working shoes she was wearing didn't do much for her feet.

She looked at her feet and said, 'And she had a very cluttered house, tidy, not a pin out of place, but a house you hardly dared move around in. I used to knock things over all the time. Right into my teens my knees and elbows wouldn't co-ordinate. I had to teach myself how to walk keeping my elbows in and watching where I put my big feet.'

Tom burst out laughing. 'Well, you've got the mechanism co-ordinated now, you're a lovely mover.'

He was amused, but he wasn't laughing at her, and she thought he might even make her smile about Barry too, when she got round to telling him that story.

Although he would probably think her a fool for
handing over her money. That wouldn't be easy to
explain, even if Tom was the easiest companion she
had ever had. She said, 'It's a pity you don't have a
sister.'

'Why?'

'You'd make a nice brother.' If she had had someone
like him all her life perhaps she wouldn't have had
this inner insecurity that made her cringe at the
sound of a raised voice. 'I could do with a brother like
you,' she said.

He said, 'Could you?' and at that moment Louise
heard the helicopter. They both listened and looked
and spotted the tiny dot in the blue sky, and watched,
without saying anything, as it came closer.

When it was hovering overhead, and there was no
doubt that this was where it was about to land, Louise
felt resentful at whoever was disturbing her peaceful
paradise, whether it was Paula, or Mary Edmunds, or
James Fenton. But whoever it was they probably had
every right to drop in, and she had no call to be sitting
here glowering.

'Visitors,' she said, although 'Owners' would be more
likely. She was the one with no claim to anything,
except to be paid when her work was done.

'Shall we let them land?' said Tom.

'I wish we had a choice,' she said wistfully.

The helicopter settled in the middle of the lawn,
and Tom got to his feet as a man climbed down from
the machine. 'James Fenton?' asked Louise. 'Well, I've
got his bedroom and his dressing room ready for him,
if he doesn't mind sleeping on the floor.'

Tom went across the grass and stood talking to the
man, who was tall and dark and rather overweight;
while Louise went along the terrace, and in through
one of the open French windows of the drawing room,

to tear off another strip of faded wallpaper.

She would be interested to see Fenton. She knew that he was in construction, head of an industry with upward of a dozen large factories, here and abroad. She had read news stories of orders for his firm, quotes he had made on industrial matters, but she didn't read the gossip columns, so she knew nothing of his private life.

She had seen Paula on television, and in the occasional film, but until she had been engaged to do this house she hadn't known that Miss Cavell was more or less living with Mr Fenton. If she had known she would have been completely uninterested, but if James Fenton was planning to make Tir Glyn his home then she would be interested in meeting him. She liked to imagine her characters in her settings, and she waited with rising anticipation for him to step into the drawing room.

When he did the room was looking very much the worse for wear, and she was half way up a ladder. 'Good morning, Mr Fenton,' she said. 'This is the first stage. I've finished a couple of rooms upstairs if you'd like to look at them.'

'I'm not Mr Fenton,' he said, and that surprised her so much that she nearly fell off the ladder.

'Who are you, then?' she gasped.

'Robert Gillian.' Did they all have helicopters? 'I—ah—work for Mr Fenton,' he said.

So Mr Fenton was engaging the staff for Tir Glyn. That was thoughtful of him. The house should be staffed and smooth-running before Miss Cavell—Mrs Fenton?—took up residence. That would be nice for her.

'You—ah—started sooner than we expected.' He looked very businesslike, in his impeccable grey suit. He had heavy features and shrewd eyes, and his hesitant speech was rather disconcerting. It made you feel that he was considering his words before he spoke them.

Louise came down the ladder, and told him, 'I spoke to Miss Edmunds.'

'Yes, I know.' Another hesitation, then, 'Everything all right? You've—ah—got everything you need?'

'Yes, thank you.'

'If not—ah,' he seemed to be trying to remember the name, 'Tom—will deal with it for you. He's—ah—in charge here.'

She thanked him again and he wished her good day.

He was in the house for quite a long time. The helicopter was on the lawn and the two men seemed to be in the study, because once the phone rang and stopped right away. Tom always answered the phone, although Louise wasn't so nervous about it now. At the end of next week, when Barry came back from holiday, she would very probably have a scene on her hands, but it was unlikely anyone would try to contact her here until then.

She was getting herself cheese and biscuits for lunch when she heard the engine start up, and she came into the hall and went to the open front door to watch the helicopter rise.

Tom had walked across the lawn with Robert Gillian, and was standing back now. Louise waved. She didn't expect the rather pompous Mr Gillian to look down, and anyway it wasn't a personal salute. She was just glad to wave him off because he reminded her that this was somebody else's house.

She went to meet Tom, to tell him that anything she needed she only had to ask, and ah—Tom would provide. Mr Gillian had said so. She thought that might amuse him, but he wasn't smiling now. He had the tight-lipped look.

'Everything all right?' she heard herself asking.

'Yes.'

'He was here a long time.'

'Plenty of instructions.'

'Oh.'

Tom was walking back towards the house and she walked with him. He was striding out as though he was in a particular hurry, and she wondered whether he was off to catch up on all those instructions. She said gaily, 'I hope they don't want you to dig a swimming pool after all.'

'Not quite.' He took her arm; he hadn't done that before unless the ground had been very rugged, and his touch always flustered her. Even the fleeting contact of handing over a cup, or him brushing casually against her as they were walking, or sitting out on the verandah bench together taking their evening meal.

She was relaxed with Tom, look how she could talk to him and joke with him. As she had just been saying when Mr Gillian came down from the skies, she wished Tom was her brother. But when he slipped his hand through her arm her mouth went so dry that her tongue stuck to the roof of her mouth.

She went on talking about Robert Gillian, as though she hardly noticed Tom's hand over hers. 'The wretched man didn't even step upstairs to see my beautiful rooms. Did he? If he'd seen them he didn't say anything to me about them.'

'Not his province,' said Tom. 'There was a phone call while we were in the study.'

Louise was suddenly apprehensive. 'I heard it ring. What about it?'

'Your boy-friend, Mason.'

She couldn't say anything at first. She knew that Barry would cause trouble. He had a big laugh, a big voice. When he was annoyed he shouted. He had never been annoyed with her before, but when he realised that she wasn't going back to him on his terms, or any terms, he could very easily shout and bluster. The thought of that made her feel sick and cold. She said, 'He's still in Spain.'

'Is he? He was on the line just now, and Gillian answered.'

'And told him I was here?'

'Yes. You didn't want to speak to him?'

'*No*! Not in front of Mr Gillian. Not at all if I could get out of it. What lousy luck!' She tried to smile, but her lips wouldn't. 'That he had to ring just then. I thought I had at least another week before he caught up with me.'

As they walked up the steps Tom said, 'If he's still in Spain you probably have. You're actually running from him?'

'Yes.'

'Why?' At the top of the steps he turned her to face him, and she said quietly,

'I want to finish.'

'Finish what? An affair? A marriage?'

'An affair, of sorts.'

'And he doesn't?'

She answered in hardly more than a whisper, 'He isn't in love with me, but I think he could be angry.'

'You think he might harm you?'

He was concerned for her. There was something glittering and dangerous in his eyes. He thought she was threatened and he would have come to her aid, and she wished she could have said 'Yes' because he would have understood that kind of fear, but she had to say 'No.'

'Then *what*?'

She said miserably, 'There'll be a scene. I hate

scenes. He'll shout.' No wonder Tom stared. Then he said slowly, .

'Are you getting yourself into this state because some man might raise his voice?'

Louise wouldn't blame him if he began to laugh, and she twisted away and went to sit on the bench, looking away, her arms folded across her breasts, gripping her elbows tightly.

She said the lot, drawing a quick shallow breath when she had to. 'I know it sounds stupid and it's cowardly and I can't explain it myself, but I can't stand rows. With some folk it's spiders or heights or being shut in or thunderstorms. That's another thing with me, thunderstorms, but I'd run a mile to avoid any sort of quarrel. If he phones again I'll speak to him, but he's the real reason I'm not going back home for a month or two, because I can't stand being shouted at.'

Then she looked back, slowly, over her shoulder, and Tom said, 'Fair enough.' He wasn't smiling. He was just standing there, looking at her.

She said, 'You don't understand. do you?'

'No.'

It was simple enough. She was a coward. She had high principles and she didn't think she had ever let anyone down—although Douglas and Barry might think she had. She treasured her friends, and she worked very hard, but she was a coward and Tom probably despised her for it. She said wryly, 'Aren't you scared of anything?'

'Not of thunderstorms or being shouted at.'

He was smiling now, and he came and sat beside her and said, 'What do you say we eat out tonight? We could use your van, or I could take you on the back of my bike.'

Louise began to say, 'All right,' and then she thought of something else and started again. 'You know what I'd really like to do? Have a meal in the dining room. The table's there.' Covered with her papers, but she could soon shift them. 'And there are chairs around.'

'Why not?' said Tom.

She smiled herself then. 'I suppose it's Mr G coming that makes me want to pretend it's my house and I can dine in the dining room any time I want.'

'And so you can.' He reached out and held her hand again, as though he was reassuring a child. 'Dine in the dining room, lounge in the drawing room, doss down in the master bedroom.'

She laughed and shook her head. 'I'd better not get too carried away with make-believe. I'd better get back to work.'

'We both had.' She stood up as he did, and he gave her hand a final squeeze that was like a pat on the head. He was right—she was childish about some things. What grown woman these days couldn't face up to the occasional slanging match?

She went back to the drawing room and carried on working until it was nearly six o'clock. Then she did her usual end-of-the-day tidy-up, and went along to the dining room. In there she cleared her papers and plans off the big table, and put them neatly into her portfolio, took the dust sheets off several assorted chairs that were stacked together against the wall, and brought two straight-backed chairs to the table. They could eat in here now, and very pleasant it would be.

The dining room had a white marble fireplace, topped by brighter wallpaper in the shape of a departed over-mirror. The wallpaper was dingy and old, peeling a little here and there. Louise was to paint the walls olive green, and the paintwork white, including the open cupboards in alcoves, skirting the fireplace. A glowing red Persian carpet would give the room a rich and elegant air, and so would the Regency furniture, of course.

She could see it as it was going to be, with its long windows overlooking the front of the house, but it was charming as it was, in spite of the bare floorboards and the patches on the walls where the mirror and the pictures had hung.

She dusted the mantelpiece, and was giving the table a vigorous rub, trying to work up a shine, when Tom arrived in the doorway.

'I can't see why they need to muck about with this room,' he said, 'it looks all right to me,' and Louise rounded on him in mock indignation.

'That's my living you're knocking, mucking about with rooms. Have you heard me say you ought to leave the garden the way it was?'

'You weren't too happy about some of the wild flowers.'

'Well, no, but they'll go on growing, won't they?'

'I think you can rely on that,' he said. 'See you for dinner in about an hour? I'm not ready yet.'

She wondered if Mr Gillian had suggested that Tom should work longer hours, and how that plumpish gentleman would have enjoyed delving through the hard earth of the kitchen garden himself.

It wouldn't take long to get the meal ready, they were only having ham and eggs, and she could do with a rest for half an hour. She was feeling jaded tonight. The phone call from Barry had drained some of her energy, and when she got into the bath she lay there, relaxing and recuperating, instead of briskly loofahing herself down and leaping out.

Tom's suggestion that they might eat somewhere else was a good idea. It was summer holiday time, there were any number of places they could drive out to for an evening meal, and it would be a break from work, a little treat. But tonight she was looking forward to eating in the dining room, although it was a silly thing to want to do.

She soaked the grime out of her skin and from under her fingernails, instead of rubbing and scrubbing, and washed her hair. Then she sat on the side of her bed, with her hand dryer, brushing and drying, with the window open and the air sweet and soft, feeling languorous and lazy, as though all her senses were soothed. If she had been a cat she would have been purring.

Her skin was very smooth after her bath, and she smiled at herself for wishing she had silk to wear. She would put on a dress for the dining room, instead of jeans, although she hadn't brought along anything but very ordinary everyday clothes.

Each previous evening here she had hurried to get downstairs to the alfresco meal on the terrace, but there was no hurry tonight, and she pampered herself, making up slowly, and smiling into the mirror to encourage herself.

Her dress was a pale blue crisp linen, short-sleeved, belted and buttoned. She had brought several scarves, for covering her hair while she was working, and she knotted the red and white spotted one round her throat.

She was not ecstatic about her appearance, by a long chalk, but she didn't look too bad. She felt that Tom might be quite impressed, that his standards wouldn't be impossibly high, and it had to be Tom she was dressing up for because there was no one else here.

She was glad Tom was on her side. When he had thought she was physically scared of Barry he would have protected her, and that was something. She had never had a champion before, someone to call on in time of trouble. Although she wasn't sure how he would react if she told him that. He probably didn't see himself as anyone's champion, just a scrapper in his own right.

When she went downstairs the table was laid for two in the dining room and there was a bottle of wine, and she exclaimed 'Wow!' Then she turned to Tom, who was at the window at the far end of the room. She was going to ask where the wine had come from, but the words died on her lips.

He was wearing black slacks, a thin black polo-necked sweater. He looked terrific—different, and sensationally attractive, and she found herself stammering, 'I—wouldn't have known you.'

He grinned, 'I'm not so sure I'd have known you.' He didn't realise she meant it. She couldn't believe herself that a change of apparel could make him look so much—well, sexier; and the answer to that was that it didn't.

The pants were well tailored, smooth-fitting over slim hips, and the sweater moved with the rippling muscles of broad shoulders, but whatever he was wearing Tom Reading was a man most women would find very exciting indeed. And so did Louise, and she knew that she had, right from the beginning, in spite of all her talk about wouldn't he make a nice brother.

'A good old tradition,' he said, 'dressing for dinner.'

He pulled out a chair for her, with a flourish, and she sat down, looking at the bottle of wine, asking, 'Where did that come from?'

'Our masters left a few bottles,' he told her gravely, and laughter surged in her.

'That's all right then. Mr Gillian did say that anything I needed ah—Tom would provide.' He grinned at her mimicry and it wasn't like it had been with

Douglas or Barry. Tom made her laugh, and she could talk to him as she had never talked to anyone else.

This week had been good, and if their relationship developed she would like that very much. By the time she had finished her work here she would have been under the same roof as Tom for four months. They said you never really knew anyone unless you had lived with them. She liked him very much and he liked her, and in the months ahead she would be happy if they grew closer.

Tonight took on the air of a celebration. It was probably the wine, and the fact that they were sitting at a large table in an elegant room, instead of gipsy fashion outside. Even ham and eggs, taken with a cool hock, seemed a gourmet dish, and they talked about all manner of things. It was a continual surprise to Louise how much Tom knew. But then he'd knocked around the world, and it was a good way to get educated.

They sat with coffee until the sun set, and a grey pearl dusk fell over the hills. There were no curtains to draw when they switched on a wall light. Eventually there would be a Regency chandelier overhead, but for now only the wall lights functioned. The light of one of those was almost as mellow as candlelight.

But at last tiredness began to catch up with Louise —it never seemed to with Tom, but she was starting to yawn. Before she went, though, she said, 'You think I'm an idiot to get churned up about Barry, don't you? To be scared that he might shout at me?'

'You could shout back.' Yes, of course, except that she couldn't. She twisted the stem of her empty wine glass between her finger tips and said,

'That's it—I just can't.'

'Did you get shouted at much as a child? This Aunt Louise of yours?'

'Goodness, *no*! Never. When she was annoyed Aunt Louise was a whisperer. She hissed.' She smiled, because Aunt Louise didn't worry her any more. She felt sorry for a woman who had never asked for love, nor given it, and Tom smiled too.

'I'm very glad I missed meeting her.' Which meant he would have expected to meet Louise's family, if she had had a family, that he didn't consider their relationship would begin and end up here in the empty old house.

She felt a warm glow, and he said, 'And don't lie awake worrying. If Barry Mason turns up after you I'll throw him out.'

He didn't mean physically, of course, and Barry wouldn't be likely to be coming all this way after her, but she was very grateful. 'It shouldn't come to that, but thank you,' she said.

She said goodnight a few minutes later, and Tom stood up when she did. 'Goodnight,' he said. He went towards the open French windows. Perhaps he closed them, perhaps he went out to walk around the grounds before he turned in.

Louise didn't wait to see. At first, when he'd stood up, she had thought he might be going to kiss her goodnight, and she had taken a couple of quick backward steps, so she had to keep on walking towards the door while he strolled across to the windows.

It wasn't that she would have found a goodnight kiss distasteful, on the contrary, but circumstances were unusual up here, and it might be unwise to rush things, because things might very easily get out of hand.

CHAPTER FOUR

NEXT morning Louise was still working on her paper-stripping in the drawing room when she heard the car, and she went to look out and watch it coming round the sweep of the drive. A red Jag, and the only red Jag she knew was Barry's. There were others, of course, but she moved back, peeping round the side of the window as it stopped below and the driver stepped out.

The sunshine glinted on his fair hair and on the bright blue tank top he had bought while she was with him, a couple of weeks ago. There was no mistaking either, it was Barry. She'd expected him to ring again, she had never thought he might arrive here without any warning at all, and her instinctive reaction was to run for Tom.

But she had no real idea where Tom was. Somewhere in the garden, probably, although he could be somewhere in the house, and she must pull herself together.

She must go and meet Barry, and however he carried on he couldn't destroy her. He couldn't really do anything, except bring back the echoes of nightmare, of angry shouting voices that sent her spiralling into black horror. If he shouted she would simply walk away. Tom might have heard the car too. Tom might be coming now.

Louise pulled the scarf off her head and went through the front door as Barry reached the bottom of the steps, and he gave a whoop of delight, as though she was the person he most wanted to see and he had no doubts at all of his welcome. He came racing up the steps and flung his arms around her, lifting her off her feet. 'Hello, hello! Surprised to see me?'

The moment he put her down she pulled loose, and stood with her arms tightly folded. 'Very,' she said. 'I thought you were in Spain.'

'I came back yesterday.' He gave her a broad winning smile. Come on now, said his smile, aren't you glad I came back yesterday?

'Why?' she asked.

'I wanted to say—sorry for what I said.' He still smiled, as though it had been hardly more than a slip of the tongue, something no reasonable woman would hold against him. Louise could hardly explain that it was less what he had said than the look which was so like Douglas, the other greedy man in her life. 'Things got a bit on top of me,' he went on. 'I suppose I needed that holiday.'

'You should have had it,' she said quietly. 'You should have stayed for the fortnight.'

He was briefly nonplussed, then he said, 'Yes—well, I'm here now, and this is the weekend, so I thought I'd come over and see how you were doing.'

'How did you know I was here?'

'You weren't home. I asked around. Everyone thought you were with me. Then I phoned here and some bloke told me you were here but you couldn't take a phone call at the moment.' He grinned. 'Were you in the bath, or aren't staff allowed phone calls in working hours?'

'I was working,' she said.

Either he didn't realise that he wasn't welcome or he had decided to ignore it. He sounded as though everything had been smoothed out and explained away. 'It's a lonely place, isn't it?' He had transferred his attention to the house, looking up at the windows that were still shuttered on the first floor, and along the empty terrace. 'And that lane coming up isn't too good on the old car springs.'

'They drop in from the skies,' Louise said drily. 'There was a helicopter on that lawn yesterday. The man who spoke to you came in it.'

'Did he?' Barry was envious. 'That's it, isn't it? The way to operate?'

'I suppose so,' she said. 'When time's their kind of money.'

The big silent house, and the vast overgrown garden, were perhaps a little eerie until you were used to them, as Louise was. Or unless you had loved the house on sight, as she had. Barry Mason was unimaginative, but it was not a place he would have cared to have been stuck in alone, and he asked, 'You're never up here on your own, are you?'

'No.'

She rubbed her cheek, as though she was brushing off a gnat or a tickling hair, because she was afraid that she was blushing slightly, although there was nothing to blush for. Now he would want to know who else was here, and she didn't want to discuss Tom. She took a deep breath and said, 'I don't know why you came. The last time I saw you you said we had no future, and you're right, we haven't.'

Barry really had believed he had Louise in the palm of his hand. He had expected she would be at the airport to catch that plane to Spain, and when she wasn't he had caught it alone in a foul temper. Even after his temper cooled down his spirits didn't improve, as he recalled what a business asset Louise had been, and that he was fond of her. She was a nice girl, the kind who would make a tolerant wife, and their friends were relieved when, after a few days, he'd decided to cut his holiday short.

They were all for him returning home and making it up with Louise. He hadn't explained what the row was about, but they were sure that Louise would be hurt at being left behind, and they liked her too.

They thought she was a nice girl, everybody did, although rather quiet and reserved. It was Barry who was usually the life and soul of the party, but this week, without Louise, Barry had been a pain in the neck. So they didn't mind at all when he packed up and left them.

He had thought Louise would still be at home or in her office. The quarrel, he told himself, had hardly been on her side at all. She had been pigheaded about not asking for the money in advance—and he was sure he could do something about that if he played it cool—but he was the one who had shot off his mouth. He was sorry now. He was ready to apologise, and when he found that she was already at work he took it for granted that she was trying to finish ahead of schedule for his sake. He had a very good opinion of himself. He thought that he looked like Ryan O'Neal.

Now he said. 'Sweetheart, what's all this about? You don't mean this.'

'But I do.'

He wouldn't believe it. 'You want to finish with me just because my business is going through a rough patch?'

That made her sound horrible. 'No,' she protested, and he said quickly,

'Things will pick up, they always do. I lost my temper, I'm sorry. What more can I say?'

He was as appealing as a contrite small boy, and Louise muttered miserably, 'It doesn't matter. What you said doesn't matter. It's just that I think we'd be better apart for a while. I'm going to be a few months on this job, and that should give us time to sort things out.'

'But we were going to get engaged in Spain.' He had felt magnanimous, very big-hearted being prepared to marry Louise, because she was hardly a raving beauty. Now he reminded her and waited for her to weaken, although if she was going to be this unco-operative he was glad he hadn't made it a firm offer.

She shook her head. 'No,' she said, and he yelped,

'What do you mean, *no*? You're turning me down?'

She had been turning him down ever since he'd arrived here, but it seemed impossible to get the message through. She said, 'You don't really want to marry me. You only want me as an unpaid service for the firm and——'

'And now you've got this commission you're setting your sights a bit higher?' he sneered, but it wasn't that simple. She had ceased to be infatuated with Barry. Although she was still prepared to help him she was not handing over any more money, and she knew quite well that was where her main attraction lay.

She begged, 'Do please go away,' and he took a couple of steps towards her. She didn't know whether he was going to take her in his arms again, or whether he was losing his temper again. He wasn't looking loving, and she backed to the top of the steps, spotting Tom coming across the lawn with immense relief.

She started to hurry down the steps towards him. 'Do come and meet Barry,' she'd say. 'He was passing this way and he looked in, but he's just leaving now, aren't you, Barry?'

But on the third step down she trod on a patch of moss and her feet shot from under her, so that she rolled and bounced and landed in an undignified and breathless heap at the bottom.

Both men shouted, and began to run towards her as she raised a groggy head, sure that she must have broken or twisted something.

Tom reached her first. He knelt down beside her and put an arm around her, asking, 'All right?' Louise was surprised to find that her arms and legs still functioned. Bruises would probably develop, but she could have fared far worse, pitching down a flight of steps like that.

'Nothing broken,' she said shakily.

They looked at one another, and to Louise in that moment everything else disappeared. Tom, holding her, shut out the rest of the world. She was only conscious of his arms, and the face that was looking concerned and glad that she wasn't hurt. But he would smile in a moment and his lips would brush her forehead, then her lips.

Barry was non-existent, until he asked, 'Who are you?'

He was standing beside them, glaring down, and Tom lifted her so that she was seated two steps up. Then he stood up and faced Barry. 'Mason?' he said.

'That's me. Who are you?'

'All through?' Tom asked Louise, and she nodded. 'On your way, then,' said Tom. He spoke softly, but there was something in his voice and his eyes that sent a chill down Louise's spine, although it was in no way directed at her.

She sat, her fingers clenched together, staring speechlessly at the two men, while it seemed that Barry shrank so that Tom was taller. Physically Barry was the bigger man but, without moving, without another word, Tom seemed to tower over him with a dominating authority.

Then Barry walked away, and Tom walked beside him. They spoke a few words Louise couldn't hear. It was very quiet. She could hear a bird singing, but she only knew the men spoke because she saw Barry's lips move when he turned his head just before he got into his car.

The car backed into a three-point turn on the flagstones of the forecourt, and went screeching off down the drive, and she tried to stand up. But she was still none too steady, so she stayed where she was, until Tom came back. Then she said, 'Thank you.'

'A pleasure.' He sat down beside her. 'You're really all right?'

'Mmm.' She touched her elbow and winced, then stretched arm and neck trying to see the damage where the skin was scraped off her elbow. She would have to wash that and dab iodine on it and it was going to smart like mad. She grimaced and said, 'You told me I was co-ordinating well these days. How was that for a great auk landing?'

He grinned. 'Not bad. What did he have to say?'

'All is forgiven.' She smiled back and wished he would put his arm around her again. But he sat, lounging on the steps.

'And what did you say?' he asked her.

'I said "Please go away". I never dreamt he'd come all this way, and what did you do to make him leave so quietly?'

'Like you, I said, "Please go away".'

'Do people always do what you tell them?'

After a moment he said, 'Yes,' and she gasped. He didn't seem to have any reservations about it. She'd expected him to say 'Sometimes', not 'Yes', like that, meaning always; and he wasn't joking or boasting either. There was no particular expression on his face. His eyes were hooded, and this was one of the times when she didn't know what to make of him.

But he had just seen Barry off for her, without any voices being raised, and she said, 'I'm glad you were here when he came.'

'It's working out well, isn't it? This partnership of ours.'

'Very well.' She hugged herself and winced again—

oh yes, there were going to be bruises, and there was a tender throbbing bump on the back of her head. She touched that very gingerly.

'You're lucky you didn't break a leg,' said Tom. 'I must do something about these steps.' Her legs seemed all right, her jeans would have protected them. She was wearing one shoe and she looked around for the other and said,

'I'd better get back to work.'

'Not right away.'

She saw her shoe, lying half way down the flight of steps. She was sure there was no need to take it easy, but she was shaken up and she did need a steady hand in her work, and a steady head for small heights.

'Sit down on the bench,' Tom advised her, 'and I'll get you a cup of tea.'

'Thank you.' Should she ask for a couple of aspirins in case her crack on the head developed into a headache? But at the moment it was only a slight ache, and she could always take a pain killer later if she needed one.

'Come on,' he said, and helped her to her feet. He collected her shoe as they went, putting it on her foot while she used his shoulder as support.

Then she sat, on the wrought iron bench, and waited for her tea, and thought that this was worth sliding down a few old steps for. She was revelling in the unaccustomed sensation of someone being really concerned about her. She had good friends who cared, and would have rushed to pick her up if they had been here, as indeed would most strangers, but with Tom it seemed very personal. Besides, there was nobody else alive whose comforting touch stirred her in this strange way.

They drank their tea slowly, not talking much. Neither said anything about Barry until Louise finished her cup, then she joked, 'I suppose I ought to have offered him a cup of tea, he'd come such a long way.'

'He didn't say he was thirsty,' said Tom, deadpan, and she laughed.

'He didn't, did he? So that's all right. I wonder who our next caller will be. Mr Gillian yesterday, Barry today. I'm a believer in the rule of three. Only it won't stop at three.'

There would be hordes coming before long, and she sighed, and Tom said, 'I wish it would myself.'

She was pleased to hear him say that. He didn't want the hordes either. He liked it as it was, just the two of them. She felt that she would never find such peace again, and as he held out a hand for her teacup she said, 'I'm fine now, I'm going back to work.'

'What are you doing, exactly?'

'I'm in there.' She looked towards the drawing room and he said,

'I know that much.' He walked with her, carrying the two teacups. They went into the room by the French windows, Louise had come out through the hall to the main door, but the windows were open on to the terrace and Tom stepped inside when she did.

The ladders and boards were in place. She was working high up, with a stubborn embossed ceiling paper, and Tom said, 'Oh no, not today.'

'I'm fine,' she insisted, although when she put her head back to look up the bump area went on throbbing. An unpleasant thought struck her, and she looked at him in trepidation. 'I might be worse tomorrow. Don't bruises and stiffness sometimes develop next day?'

'Usually,' he said cheerfully.

'But I can't afford to stiffen up. It would be awful if I had to hobble up and down my ladders. And please don't smile!' she wailed. His lips were twitching. It might be comic, the thought of her contortions as she tried to decorate this room, but she wasn't finding it funny.

He said, 'There's a first aid cupboard in the bathroom I'm using, let's get you rubbed down,' and she said,

'You make me sound like a horse,' because that embarrassed her. Suppose he took it for granted she needed someone to help apply the liniment how, without sounding old-fashioned and prudish, could she explain that she was too skinny to enjoy displaying herself? And that she was so inhibited that stripping off in front of him, even retaining the essentials of coverage, would reduce her to scalding shyness?

He said, 'There's probably something around for horses too, if you'd prefer that,' and she laughed and waited to see what he would come back with. She didn't feel up to rushing around. She might take it easy for a while. There was plenty she could do without climbing ladders; she might start stripping the paintwork.

And now she reflected on her situation she had been lucky. She could have broken a leg or an ankle; or got a bad sprain that would have incapacitated her. She had walked down those steps dozens of times, she knew where the slippery spots were, but just now she had been hurrying to get to Tom, so that he would come and deal with Barry for her.

He came back with a jar, reading the instructions on the side which promised relief from—among other things—the muscle aches and sprains of unaccustomed exercise. 'How's that sound to you?' he asked. 'Do you often come head first down from terraces?'

'It's a habit I'm trying to break,' she said gravely.

She went up to 'her' bathroom, and applied the stuff

liberally on her joints—all except the scraped elbow—
and rubbed it in as best she could. It warmed up when
it sank below the surface, the burning sensation
swamping the aching, and she hoped it was doing her
good, but she didn't care for the smell of it.

She dressed again and went downstairs, and out
again on to the terrace. Tom was scraping the moss
from the steps, which wasn't easy because the steps
were uneven, cut from natural rock. They were never
going to be steps that anyone should trip down in a
hurry. When Barry came bounding up them he didn't
realise what a risk he was taking.

Tom put down the trowel and came up to her and
she said, 'I'm covered with it. Now I'll *have* to work
with the windows open.'

'There's grit in that elbow.'

'Is there?' She made another attempt to examine it,
she should have checked in the bathroom mirror. 'I
can't see,' she said.

'I'll bathe it for you.'

She would have said, 'I think I'd rather dab at it
myself,' but he didn't give her a chance to object. He
walked along with her to the kitchen, and while she
was saying, 'I'll manage, I'll use a mirror,' he had a
cotton wool swab and a bowl of warm water laced with
disinfectant.

Of course it hurt. It wasn't deep but it was messy, and
the dirt was embedded, and although he held her arm
gently, and bathed it gently too, and she kept her head
turned away, it hurt enough to bring tears to her eyes.

He put on ointment, something soothing, and a pad
of lint secured by a criss-cross of adhesive tape. Then
he put an arm around her and said, 'Don't cry.'

'I'm not.' Her eyes were watering, and she blinked
them, and thought that she couldn't remember anyone
before holding her in their arms and saying, 'Don't

cry.' Not even when she was a baby and her parents were dead.

'Will you do something for me?' said Tom.

'Of course.'

'I want you to take the rest of the day off.' Louise parted her lips to protest and he went on, 'I don't want you working any more today. Please.'

'All right.' She would sit in the sunshine and talk to him. After all, it was Sunday, and she was entitled to a break. Perhaps in a little while he would stop working too, and they could take the rest of the day off together. The sea was only a mile or two away. They might go to the sea. She smiled, 'No one ever told me to stop work before.'

'You need someone to look after you.'

'Don't we all?' she said huskily.

He touched her hair, and she felt even that light touch in every nerve. 'This partnership of ours,' he said, 'I'd like to talk about it with you.'

'Yes?'

'Later.' He stroked her hair very gently, but she winced and he took his hand away. 'When the bump on your head's gone down,' he said. 'I don't want any unnecessary confusion.'

'Who's going to be confused?'

He smiled, and she wondered if he meant they might go on working together, but 'take care of you' he had said, so it had to be more personal than that. She said, 'I said you'd make a nice brother.'

'I wouldn't make a nice anything.' He tilted her chin, the dark eyes and the hard straight mouth swam above her. 'You're not that confused, are you? You can't see me as your big brother?' Her lips framed, 'No'. 'Any more than I see you as sister Louise,' he said, and he kissed her, lightly, swiftly, sensuously.

She had no time to kiss him back, nor even to hold

on to him. It was over in a moment, but it left her senses whirling, and she leaned against the low wall of the terrace, trying to get back her breath without gasping aloud.

Tom looked down again at the steps. 'I need something to shift this stuff,' he said. 'It's no good hacking at it.'

'Moss-killer?' she suggested, in a normal casual voice that surprised her.

'There might be some about.'

'With the horse embrocation, in the first aid box?' she said gaily, and he grinned,

'Could be.' He went, to search around in the outhouses and garden sheds for moss-killer, and Louise seated herself on the terrace wall.

The sun was hot and high overhead, so that the house threw little shadow. She wasn't sure whether she was more shaken by her fall, or by what Tom had just said and that kiss. He was a very disturbing man. She had only known him a week, everything was much slower with Douglas and Barry. Tom was different. Tom was probably more dangerous.

Sometimes his force of personality was like a body blow. Look at the way Barry had crumpled. There was some quality Louise couldn't fathom in Tom, something leashed, held back. What? Violence? Suppressed violence? She shivered a little at that, although it was so warm, sitting here in the sun. He was kind, but he could be frightening, and she couldn't have said why.

She put a hand in front of her eyes and thought she might do better to get inside out of the sun, or at least put her scarf on her head. She heard Tom's footsteps on the terrace and looked up and smiled, and he said, 'You're pale.' It sounded like an accusation.

'My lipstick's worn off, and I think the fumes of this stuff have gone to my head.' Of course she wasn't afraid of him. What she felt for him was a long way from fear. 'Like the Delphic Oracle, wasn't it?' she said lightly. 'Who got high on volcanic fumes and told everybody's fortune.'

He laughed. 'Ah, it's a grand thing to have a classical education. I think you should lie down for an hour.'

Perhaps she should. She assured him, 'I'm not concussed, just shaken. But if I do lie down for an hour will you stop work and take me to the sea?'

'I will,' he said.

So she went up to her little room, and got out of her jeans and shirt, and lay on the bed staring up at the ceiling.

She was falling in love with Tom, more deeply than she had ever expected to fall in love. When Douglas and Barry had failed her she had felt miserable, and thought that the heartache might be a breaking heart, but it had been nothing of the sort. She hadn't run much risk with either of them, but it would be a risk with Tom.

It had to be, after only a week. There had to be so much she didn't know about him. She didn't even know how he felt about her, except that he had kissed her and some time they were going to discuss this partnership of theirs.

They were going to the seaside in a little while, and she stopped staring at the ceiling, and closed her eyes and saw a seashore instead. A cove under the cliffs with no one else about, seagulls wheeling and waves lapping gently on the shingle.

It was such a pleasant reverie that it lulled her asleep, and for a while she went on with the dream. Then, still in her dream, the sky changed. A single fluffy white cloud spread and darkened at a terrifying speed, and she was alone and lightning was filling the sky and thunder was crashing, until both light and sound combined into a high screaming and she woke whimpering.

The sky was blue through the window, and the shrill insistent note was the phone ringing. Louise lay and listened to it. She was glad it had woken her, she could do without dreams of thunderstorms. She waited for Tom to answer, but the ringing went on, so he couldn't hear it, and it was probably important.

She grabbed her cotton housecoat that doubled as a dressing gown, and slipped into it as she hurried down to the study. When Paula Cavell moved in there would probably be extensions all over the place, but right now there was just the one phone, down in the study. Not even in the hall. The master of this house, whoever he was, had had priority.

It must have been ringing for several minutes, and she was going to apologise. She picked up the phone from the old green leather-topped desk and began, 'Hello, this is——' when Barry cut in,

'I know who it is.'

She wasn't apologising to him. She asked wearily, 'Where are you?'

'Don't worry,' he said, 'I'm on my way home. I stopped for a bite to eat and I thought I'd give you a ring.'

He'd stopped for a drink too, by the sounds of him, and he was driving a fast car. Louise said, 'Be careful. Watch what you're drinking.' Perhaps that wasn't tactful, and he responded with heavy sarcasm.

'That is really thoughtful of you. A fat lot you'd care if I wrapped the car round the nearest tree and myself with it.'

'Please don't talk like that.' That was how her parents had died.

'How did you do it, that's what I'd like to know?

How did you get him so steamed up about you?'

She said quietly, 'I don't know what you mean.'

'A bloody millionaire.'

'*What?*'

'Fenton.' She couldn't understand. She stared blankly as Barry babbled on, 'I didn't recognise him at first. Well, he wasn't dressed like that when I saw him, was he? You don't expect the James Fentons to turn up looking like the odd job man. But when we reached the car he said, 'I can't stop you phoning or writing to her but keep off my property,' and then it dawned on me.

'I said, "You're Fenton, aren't you?" and he said, "Yes".'

Louise couldn't say a word. She was dumb, with the telephone pressed against her ear. She didn't want to hear any more, but she was a captive frozen audience.

'A cosy little set-up,' sneered Barry. 'Just you and him. I thought you'd never met him before.' When he got no reply he said bitterly, 'You're the deep one. My God, you are! You'd got me fooled all right. Well, I'll see you some time, I suppose.'

The phone clicked and so did Louise's brain, slipping back into working order. She sat down, and stared at the phone, now quiet and harmless on its cradle. Her first thought was—what nonsense; he's tight, he's rambling.

Or perhaps that bit about 'my property' had been a bluff on Tom's part. Perhaps he had actually said 'this property', and then he had just let Barry think he was Fenton.

But Barry had met Fenton before. Well, he hadn't exactly met him, but he'd seen him close to at a trade fair; and if Tom was that much like Fenton wouldn't he have mentioned it to Louise, said, 'We look alike, we could be mistaken for each other'?

If he *was* James Fenton where was Tom Reading, the caretaker whom Mary Edmunds had told her was in residence up here? And what was the point of it?

If he was Fenton ... She pulled the top drawer open slowly. Tom was in here quite a lot. She knew he used the old desk, she had supposed he had papers to deal with, things to do with the gardens, the house. Mr Gillian had told her he was in charge of the house, and when Mr Gillian had arrived they had been in this room for a long time.

What kind of papers were in this desk?

There was nothing at all about the gardens. Not a single household account. But there were some hefty reports, and letters with notes and memos scribbled in the margins. Pages initialled J.F. There was no sign that this was the desk Tom Reading used, but plenty of proof that James Fenton had been here.

There should have been other proof too. Little things, right from the beginning, ought to have made her suspicious. Like him peeling an apple that first night. What gardener peels an apple before he eats it, when the skin is sound and unblemished? She remembered the hands peeling that apple, with the little sharp knife, and knew they should have been more gnarled. They weren't the hands of a man who habitually works with his hands.

And now she knew what it was she couldn't put a name to before. It wasn't suppressed violence that made him seem dangerous. It was power. Power and the supercharged energy to be a millionaire in his early thirties.

So why was he calling himself Tom Reading? And what did he think he was going to do with her? And what, in heaven's name, was she going to do herself?

She went back to her room. The front door was open

and light streamed into the hall, and if Tom—Fenton—whoever he was—had appeared she would have told him what Barry had just said. He'd admitted his identity to Barry, he'd known all along that this couldn't last more than a day or two, so what *was* the idea?

He'd made a fool of her. He must have found that amusing. He'd probably tell the tale around. To Paula perhaps.

At the thought of Paula a pang of pain shot through her. She closed her bedroom door and sat down on the bed, her hands pressed hard together. She must not get emotional. The partnership would have been platonic, some business arrangement.

When they had got down to discussing it he would have said who he was. He must have decided she was worth backing professionally, and wasn't that something? Hadn't she hoped that this commission would be the real start to her career?

He had kissed her, but what was a kiss? Especially a kiss like that, over so soon. He'd hardly be planning to start an affair so near his marriage to Paula, with a girl who would be seeing and talking to Paula.

Louise was thankful, she knew. It would have been a horrible shock when she had expected someone called Tom to say, 'I love you,' for someone entirely different to say, 'You're good at your job, how about working for me?'

But she had a feeling of loss, a little like the time her aunt sent her dolls' house and her make-believe family to the jumble sale. She had just lost a make-believe love, and she had to stay composed and not show her feelings. She was good at that. She had had a lot of practice.

When Tom knocked on the door she was wide awake, but she pretended she had been sleeping.

'Come in,' she called, after a moment. He stood at the foot of the bed and asked,

'How are you?'

'Fine.'

'You're still looking pale.'

She was lying on top of the white candlewick coverlet, still wearing her white cotton housecoat. 'Because I'm still without make-up,' she said.

'Are you ready to go down to the beach?'

Why not? She would go along and hear what he had to say, and wait for his explanation why he had pretended to be someone else. It should be worth waiting for, that explanation.

'Give me five minutes,' she said.

She put on the dress she had worn last night, and the red scarf, and she applied lipstick and glosser. She felt utterly washed out, so she gave herself an extra measure of colour, and then went downstairs to where he was waiting.

He had brought her van out of the garage. He was only supposed to have a bike, and she wondered what he would say if she asked, 'What do you usually drive, Mr Fenton?'

She wondered if there was an old bike about, and if he could ride it, as she took the passenger seat. 'You drive,' she said. It had been shock on shock today and it was easier to sit still than to negotiate the twists and turns of the narrow lane. She had too much on her mind to concentrate on the road.

She closed her eyes and pretended to be relaxing, and she felt his scrutiny more than once. She was conscious of his every move, but she kept her eyelids closed, even when the car took a sharp right-hand turn at the bottom of the lane, and the road became rough, and the scents of flowers and grass and hedgerows were overlaid by the salt smell of the sea.

She heard the waves lapping on the shore and she wanted to look, but she didn't open her eyes until they stopped.

'Awake?' he asked. He knew that she had been awake all the time.

It was exactly the tiny cove Louise had imagined when she was daydreaming, before she slept and the phone rang and everything was spoiled. The car was on shingle. Cliffs half encircled the bay, and there were rocks and rock pools, and sea birds and sea breakers flecked with foam. There was no one else about. They had it all to themselves, with the sun shining and the sky a burning blue.

He held out a hand and she took it, because it would have looked odd if she hadn't, and they walked over the scrunching sands until they reached a large rock that threw a shadow. He sat beneath its shade and drew her down beside him and said, 'All right? Up to that discussion?'

'About our business partnership?' She looked out over the sea. 'Oh, I think so.'

There was a boat out there and she watched it intently, with a little frown that deepened when he said, 'Business? Possibly. But I wasn't thinking about business.'

She knew what he was thinking and her face flamed. She was being propositioned, and how *could* he? Goodness knows why a man with his opportunities was fancying her, but it was no compliment, knowing she knew Paula. It meant that she was someone of whom Paula would not be jealous, either a very brief encounter or one who would gratefully accept secrecy and staying in the background.

She said, coolly and bluntly, 'What are you suggesting, then, an affair?' and she made herself look straight at him.

'No?' He raised an eyebrow, and she knew he was laughing at her. He thought she was gauche, and of course he was right, and she scrambled to her feet.

'No, thank you,' she said. 'I'm sure you don't usually have this trouble with your girl-friends, but it isn't for me. It would get much too complicated and I don't think——'

She was going to say, 'I don't think Miss Cavell would approve,' when he said, 'I'm asking you to marry me.'

CHAPTER FIVE

BARRY was mistaken. He had to be. James Fenton would never have said that, but Tom might have done. Although it was a crazy thing for anyone, proposing marriage after only a week.

He was waiting now, looking at her, and he wasn't smiling, he wasn't joking. Then he said, 'Will you?' and she heard herself answer.

'Yes.' That was impulsive, and maybe idiotic, and she wasn't impulsive. It was as though someone else was answering for her. She had misgivings, this was too rushed, but somehow she said it again. 'Yes, I will.'

He smiled and looked younger. 'Now it's confession time,' he said. And the sound of the sea seemed suddenly louder, as though the waves were crashing over her instead of gently lapping the shingle.

'I'm James Fenton,' said Tom.

'*No!*' She didn't want him to be anyone but Tom, and her denial was anguished. 'You can't be, you're joking. You're the gardener—you told me.' Then she shut up, because he was telling her something else now, and she had to accept it. After a few seconds she said, 'Why?'

'Why did I say I was Tom Reading?'

'Yes.'

'I didn't want it to get around that I was here.'

She was bewildered. 'Who would I be telling?' and he suggested,

'Paula? Mary Edmunds?'

Louise bit her lip. 'Why don't you want Miss Cavell to know?'

'Because Paula and I are through. There's no more talking to be done.' He spoke in quiet tones that expressed no regret, no emotion at all. He leaned back relaxed, against the rock. His hand lay near her hand, but she couldn't have touched him. Although he had just asked her to be his wife he seemed unapproachable. She ran the tip of her tongue between her dry lips and wondered if she was really listening to this or if she could still be asleep.

'I came down to decide what I was going to do with this place,' he said. 'Put it back on the market or turn it into an hotel or live in it.' He added, as he might have explained to a business colleague, 'I'm opening a factory in Wales towards the end of the year. Prefabricated concrete.'

Prefabricated concrete? What could she say about that? 'Oh,' she said, and then, 'Tir Glyn belongs to you? I thought Miss Cavell owned it.'

This smile didn't take a single year off his age. It was tight-lipped and cynical. 'I was never quite that besotted with Paula. Nor do I feel inclined to hand Tir Glyn over as a parting gift.'

So it was his house, although Paula had been choosing the room designs. And now that affair was over, and they were no longer planning to marry. Mary Edmunds hadn't known when Louise spoke to her on the phone. She had said that Paula would be delighted that Louise was starting work early, and the house would be ready sooner. She said, 'Mary said the caretaker was here.'

'Gwyn Owen. He's got the farm just where you turn off the road.'

So the caretaker lived there and kept an eye on the house. 'Not Tom Reading?' she said.

'No.'

'Why did you choose that name?'

He shrugged. 'It was the first to come into my head.

'There isn't a Tom Reading?'

'Not to my knowledge.'

There must be hundreds, neither surname nor first name was that uncommon, but none of them was the man she knew, and again came that feeling of loss. With it the little aches and pains of her fall came creeping back, the soreness of her elbow, the throbbing bump on her head. She stared at him, back to the really puzzling matter. 'You asked me to marry you? Why on earth did you do that?'

'I need a wife.' He looked at her with his dark eyes and she could only stare back. 'And you need someone to look after you.'

'That's charitable of you,' she said doubtfully, because James Fenton would hardly be marrying for charity, and he smiled, more like his old self, like Tom.

'And I think we'd make a good partnership. You said you'd like to live in Tir Glyn.'

'Who wouldn't?' she said. 'And I suppose Tir Glyn will need a resident hostess, but that isn't my line of country.'

He overrode that objection. 'You can go on with your work. You'd get better opportunities as my wife, a wider scope. I'll back you financially and promote you.'

It sounded marvellous, but it still didn't make sense. She asked him, 'But why *me*? There must be so many women who——' and again he cut in.

'Who'd marry Fenton Structures? Yes, I suppose there are, but you said you'd marry Tom Reading.'

There was no Tom Reading, and she knew nothing at all of this man. Everything he had told her was suspect because he was playing a part. Except that no one said 'No' to him. Louise believed that.

'I enjoyed being Tom,' he said. 'I wish this week could have lasted longer.' He picked up her hand and she let her fingers lie still as his fingertips gently caressed her palm, her wrist. She was so tense that her skin felt hardly any sensation, although her bones ached.

'I'm tired of cheats and hangers-on,' he said. 'You've worked for everything you've ever had. I admire your honesty and your integrity.'

He said nothing about love. If he had been offering her a job in his organisation he would have been looking for honesty and integrity, and she said, 'I don't see this working.'

'Why not give it a chance?' He must take risks every day of his life, but she was a careful girl and she said, 'We're talking about marriage.'

'And I think it has a good chance, but if it doesn't work out it won't be the end of the world.' He didn't look on marriage as she did, that was obvious.

'I don't know,' she said desperately. 'I don't even know you do I?' He grinned,

'Maybe that's as well,' and she found herself with the ghost of a smile. 'That's better,' he said approvingly, but Louise wasn't smiling inside. She was scared and confused. He was very much in control.

'I have to be in London tomorrow,' he went on. 'The next two weeks are solidly booked. Then I've got a month's sales tour. We could get married and you could come with me.' He went through the itinerary like a holiday brochure: 'Paris, Brussels, Amsterdam and Hamburg. It wouldn't be much of a honeymoon but you did say you wanted to travel.'

She could only croak, 'That means we'd get married in a fortnight?'

'Yes. Where do you want to get married?' He was taking it for granted, taking her for granted. She should be protesting, but she said,

'At home, I suppose.' That was where she had thought she would marry Barry, some time. She couldn't marry this man in two weeks, her way of life would change completely if she became this man's wife, but she heard herself say, 'I'd have to go back. There are things I'd have to do.'

'I'll take you back in the morning.'

'On your bicycle?' She managed an unsteady smile.

'Not quite.'

He was smiling easily at her, but all her inhibitions were back. He was a stranger again, only this time she knew him to be a powerful, successful man. She was meeting James Fenton for the first time and she couldn't think of anything to say except, 'I suppose your father wasn't a gardener?'

'Up to a point. It wasn't his living.'

'What was?'

'Fenton Structures.' The firm, of course. James Fenton had been luckier in his inheritance than Barry Mason. He had prospered in every way.

Louise swallowed, her throat was very dry. 'Do you have a family?' she asked.

'No.'

She couldn't think of anything else, although there were a hundred questions she should be asking. She made a helpless little gesture. 'I'm sorry, I feel tongue-tied, stupid. I can't adjust.'

'Is it that much of a shock?'

'Yes,' she said, and added wryly, 'Maybe my head would be cooler if I hadn't had the bump on it.'

'Too much confusion for one day?' His grin was quick and sympathetic. 'I should have told you sooner. I'm sorry.'

That was two men who had said sorry to her today. What would Barry make of her marrying James Fenton? Everybody she knew would have the surprise of their lives, and nobody would be more surprised than she would herself.

He got up, holding out a hand to her. 'Come on.'

'Where?' She was hauled to her feet.

'To have a meal. And celebrate.'

She almost asked, 'Celebrate what?' That they were getting married? But she didn't believe they were. He couldn't be serious; and if he was, for the moment, something would change his plans. She had just been asked to marry a millionaire and she would have been happier if he had been a gardener.

Not that it wouldn't be marvellous to marry a millionaire, of course, but she would have had so much fun with Tom. She could have fallen unreservedly in love with him, because there would have been a chance that she could become the most important thing in his life.

Her mind boggled at the thought of all the things James Fenton must have on his mind, but it was pretty sure that if she dropped dead at his feet right now he would have almost forgotten her in a month's time.

Tom and James were two very different men. She asked huskily, 'What do I call you?'

'Whatever you like.' He was steering her back towards the van, not holding her, just guiding her along.

'Does everyone call you James?' she asked.

'Not everyone.' Well, she hadn't meant *everyone*, she'd meant the folk who were on first name terms. 'But that's my name.'

She couldn't call him Tom any more, and it wouldn't be easy to call him James. She would almost have preferred Mr Fenton, which would be ridiculous after he'd asked her to marry him. She would have to practise James when she was alone, until she could use it naturally.

As she settled into the passenger seat she asked, 'Who is Mr Gillian?' He must have been in the conspiracy, with his 'ah—Tom'.

'My P.A.'

No wonder the poor man had been ill at ease! He had known that Louise was being made a fool of, he must have felt a bit of a fool himself. 'Where would you like to go?' she was being asked, and she shrugged.

'I don't know anywhere round here. I only came down with Mary Edmunds for a couple of days. I didn't leave Tir Glyn.'

She tried to contribute something to the conversation, but she knew that she was dull company. He talked. No wonder he had seemed so knowledgeable and she tried, but she couldn't chatter to James Fenton. It was no use telling herself that he must have found her entertaining enough when he was pretending to be Tom, or he would hardly have asked her to marry him, because that was the most unrealistic part of the whole situation.

She could have sworn that she was boring him now When the silences fell, and he waited to see if she was going to break them, his sidewards glance at her seemed cool and speculative.

'Let's try here,' he said, and parked her van in the forecourt of an opulent hotel. He was dressed in the

brown check shirt and brown trousers, she was in jeans
and shirt, with her elbow sticking-plastered; and she
wouldn't have been surprised if they had either been
refused admission—too late for lunch—or seated well
back in the dining room.

She stood, just inside the foyer, while Tom went to
the reception desk. It was cool in here, out of the sunshine. The walls were latticed in green with a silver
background, and Louise began to decorate the whole
place again, in her mind's eye. Not because it wasn't
attractive for a hotel foyer, but because work was the
easiest thing to think about.

Some folk repeated a mantra when they were
troubled, others did deep breathing or counted slowly
to ten. Louise designed rooms. That kept her looking
calm and stopped her thinking about anything else.

Like slipping outside and getting into her van and
getting away. She had come down here hoping to
escape from trouble for a while, and found herself in a
much more puzzling and explosive situation than the
one that had centred round Barry.

So she concentrated on colour schemes until James
Fenton touched her shoulder. 'All right?' he said.

'Yes.'

They had a very good table, although the place was
fairly full. And such attentive service that she asked, 'I
suppose you don't own this place?'

'No. Why?'

'Do they know you?'

'No.'

He was puzzled. He didn't realise that they could
have been put at the little table by the door into the
kitchen, instead of at a window looking out over the sea.
Or that waiters don't always materialise so promptly
when you look around for them. He was James Fenton, and this was how life was for him, no matter what

kind of clothes he was wearing. He took compliance for granted. He had an inborn authority that other people accepted.

She saw the way they looked at him. Perhaps some of them recognised him. If he was opening a factory in Wales he must have been down here, but he'd said not in this hotel. He was Somebody, that was the explanation, and Louise drank a couple of glasses of crisp white wine and tried to relax.

There were mirrored panels in the dining room, in which she could see her own reflection, and she wished that she had made herself a little more presentable. She had thought they were going down to the beach, and she had had Barry's phone call on her mind, wondering what James Fenton's explanation was going to be. She hadn't even brushed her hair or made up her face.

I'm plain, she thought. It would cost a fortune to make anything of my looks. He had a fortune, the man sitting opposite her, who had asked her to marry him in two weeks' time, but of course it wouldn't happen...

They heard the phone ringing as they came round the drive towards the front of the house, and he stopped the van at the bottom of the steps. Louise wondered if it was Barry again, and hoped he had reached home safely although she didn't want to talk to him.

'I'll see who it is,' James said.

She sat there, waiting to see if he would come out again and call, 'It's for you!'

She looked at the house, and wondered how Paula Cavell was feeling at losing it. She had been full of plans, delighted at the prospect of the beautiful house it was going to be. 'My house', she had called it, and Miss Cavell didn't seem a woman who would let anything slip through her fingers. Not a house like this.

not a man who was as filthy rich as James Fenton.

If he did marry another woman she would have a bitter enemy in Paula Cavell, but Louise didn't feel personally involved. She didn't believe it would be her. She sat, with the car window wound right down, looking at the house and wondering what would happen to it, and what would happen to her job if it was going back on the market.

Would he want all the rooms painted and papered, when new owners would have their own ideas and it might be so much wasted money and effort? She would get compensation, of course, payment would be worked out, but she had wanted the house as a show-place to bring her more custom, and the best possible thing would be if he and Paula Cavell made it up again and Paula came to live here.

A shiver went through her, as though the day was turning cool, although not a leaf stirred. Somebody was walking over her grave, unless the shiver meant that she didn't want Paula coming to Tir Glyn after all.

James came out of the front door that had been left open, and she opened the car door, she thought it probably was a call for her. She was a little stiff getting out and he was down the steps before she reached them.

'Are you prepared to leave now?' he asked her.

'Now?' she echoed.

'That was Robert Gillian. If I run you back home now, I can leave first thing in the morning.'

'Leave where?' She was sounding stupid, and he was sounding impatient.

'Leave your place to get me to London. That's where I have to be in the morning.'

'I can get myself home.'

'I don't want you driving.' Neither, it seemed, did

he want her staying here. She was being pushed around, but she wasn't up to being obstructive.

'I'll pack,' she said.

She went up to the room she had been using, and put her things in her case. She wasn't looking forward to the ride, tomorrow morning would have suited her much better than today. She could have stretched out her aching bones on this little bed, and a hot bath would have been nice too. She supposed he wouldn't be prepared to hang about while she had a bath.

She carried her case downstairs. James was in the study. The door was open and she heard him on the phone. He put it down as she reached the door and said, 'Ready?'

'I suppose so.'

'You can rest in the back.'

'I'll enjoy that.' He didn't seem to notice her touch of irony. He had a suitcase and a large black bulging briefcase, and they walked through the hall in silence, and out through the front door.

Her van had vanished. In its place stood a Jensen, gleaming and powerful. Louise walked slowly down the steps, while he stacked the cases and his briefcase in the boot, and asked, 'Where did this come from?'

'It's been in an outhouse.'

It reflected her hand when she touched it. 'If I'd peered in through that window I'd have been surprised,' she said. She wasn't surprised to see it now. Everything was unreal. Even when James opened the door and she stepped in it was like watching a play, although she did point out, 'I need my van to get me around.'

'I'll have it sent down.'

'But of course.'

They stopped at the little farmhouse at the bottom of the hill, and James Fenton told Mrs Gwyn Evans, who answered the door, that the house was unoccupied again and Mr Evans was back on duty. She was a round-faced woman, who smiled first at James and then at the back window of the car, from which Louise looked out.

Louise wondered what the Evans had been told. They must have known that this was James Fenton, but probably not that he was masquerading as Tom Reading. If they knew she was up there, and tradesmen delivering had seen her, goodness knows who or what they thought she was. She had a lunatic longing to lean out and call, 'He asked me to marry him this morning. Haven't I done well?'

It was a quiet trip. She was glad she was in the back seat. If she had been shoulder to shoulder she would have felt that she had to talk sometimes, and she still couldn't think of much to say. James made a few comments at first, mostly about the countryside they were passing through, but most of the journey was in silence.

He was an excellent driver, and she watched the scenery because it was less disturbing than the back of his head. He had a thatch of thick dark hair. She supposed Paula had stroked it. Paula Cavell had beautiful hands, with pink nails oval and pretty as sugared almonds. Louise looked at her own hands and couldn't imagine them, in any circumstances, stroking James Fenton's hair.

He had asked her to marry him because he said he needed a wife, and she had integrity. It sounded a chilly arrangement, but he didn't mean a marriage without sex. He had said nothing about love, but if she was his wife he would expect a physical relationship.

She had been falling in love with Tom, but with James Fenton it would be like giving herself to a stranger, and she didn't think she could face it.

If he suggested they married in six months and got to know each other first then it would have been different, but two weeks was no time at all, especially as he wasn't even going to be around for the two weeks. He was off in the morning and then, presumably, he would meet her to marry her.

That was crazy. Of course he wouldn't. He was playing another game. She went on watching the scenery, and music played over the soft purr of the engine. When she had rattled up to Wales in her little van she certainly hadn't expected to be driven back in this style, but on the whole she might have had more peace of mind if she had been driving herself back in her little van.

As they reached her home town she prepared to give instructions on reaching her house, but James turned into the parking area of the town's biggest hotel. 'I'm booked in here,' he told her. 'I won't be long.'

That was a relief. He'd said he would be leaving her place in the morning and she'd presumed he'd expected her to put him up. He might have been taking it for granted they would be sharing a bed, and there was only the one bedroom, but Louise had a king-size sofa and that was what she would have offered him.

She was glad though to be spared the embarrassment of pleading a headache, even if she did have a bump on the head to back it up. And trying to explain that she had old-fashioned principles would have been even more difficult.

He came back without bag or briefcase, and from then on she did have to point the way. She also pointed out her office as they went through the square. 'The end window over the shop.' They were in slow-moving traffic and he had time to glance up.

'It's small,' she said, 'but it's big enough. I don't have any staff.'

She had told him that before, and she wondered what his offices looked like. When he had asked her what kind of room she would design for him she had suggested something rugged along the log cabin line. Now she could see him behind a modern desk in a modern office, running his industrial empire. Or back at the house, when everything was in place, but as master there.

'I'm home,' she said. 'Two of those windows are mine.'

He drew up in the road, and carried her suitcase up the stairs. There were two letters, and a picture post-card, on the mat. Either one of her fellow lodgers had delivered them, or Barry had collected them from the hall when he came searching for her yesterday.

She recognised the writing on the letter and card—two friends; she would read them later. The third was an electricity bill. James was looking around.

'It suits me,' she said. 'It's labour-saving. Can I get you a coffee?'

He reached and drew her towards him and instinctively she stiffened, but he didn't kiss her. He smiled instead and said. 'I've a hell of a lot of work to get down to tonight. It might be better if I went back to the hotel and saw you in the morning before I left.'

'I've got things to do too. I'll be here in the morning of course.' She spoke quickly, probably sounding un-flatteringly relieved. and she blundered on, 'If you've got a busy week ahead you'll need a good night's sleep,' and then blushed scarlet at the implications of that.

He said, 'Yes,' and kissed her as he had on the ter-race at Tir Glyn, a light brief kiss, but his mouth stirred her blood. James Fenton would have all the experience in the world, he would be able to make any caress count and be remembered. 'I'll see you tomorrow,' he said, and Louise nodded, and he left her there, standing in the middle of her living room, wondering what had hit her.

She was not taking this marriage proposal seriously, and by the time he came round in the morning she expected that he would have had second thoughts. If he hadn't she would say, 'I can't think why you think I could make the kind of wife you need, because I couldn't.' Although everybody would say she was an utter fool, missing a chance like this, the risk of unhappiness was too great.

If she let him down he could make her life hell. She would be terrified to marry a man with so much power, scared out of her wits, and she wouldn't even think about it, because it wasn't going to happen.

She made herself a strong cup of tea and sat down to read her letter. It was from a girl who had been at school with her and was now married and living fifty miles away, and who thought Louise—as an interior decorator—was leading a thrilling life. Susan, with twins of eighteen months, was finding her life restricting and warned Louise against getting married, even though Barry was so good-looking and so super.

Louise thought wryly that she should have plenty of news to fill her next letter to Susan. 'You stay single if you know what's good for you,' Susan had scribbled, although next time she would proudly enclose snapshots of the twins and be quite content with her lot.

The holiday postcard had been sent by a couple for whom Louise had done a room, and with whom she had stayed friendly.

She had made a number of friends through her work. It would be nice if she could stay friends with James Fenton. Even if he didn't want her to finish his house he might recommend her to other clients, and even if he didn't she would like to be friends.

She unpacked, undressed, and put on her housecoat over bra and pants. Then she sat on the sofa because she was still aching a little and tired. There wasn't anything she much wanted to do with the rest of today, so she would just relax and read until bedtime.

When bedtime came her head didn't ache any more, but she had to be careful how she placed it on the pillow. And her elbow was sore if she leaned on it.

She tried to keep James out of her mind, but of course there was no way she could. The events of the day kept crowding back and altogether she didn't sleep too well. She was drinking her breakfast cup of tea, still in her housecoat, when the doorbell rang.

Robert Gillian stood on the landing, and Louise blinked at him when she opened the door.

'May I—ah—come in? A lady downstairs told me to come up.'

He looked a highly respectable caller, although her downstairs neighbour might have wondered what brought him here, at half past eight in the morning. So did Louise. He was alone, and once inside the living room he produced a letter and said, 'James sends his apologies, Miss Latham, but he had to leave extremely early.'

She took the envelope with a slight smile. She had thought James would have turned up personally to say what he had to say. She expected the letter would be a delaying tactic, but when she opened it she found a sizeable cheque enclosed.

So she was being paid off, either professionally or as compensation for not becoming Mrs James Fenton, and she turned away to read the letter.

The writing was in a strong clear hand, but it looked as though it had been written fast, dashed off.

'Dear Louise, I have to be in London by ten this morning, so I won't be able to see you before I go. I suggest the ninth of next month at eleven o'clock at your local register office, if this is convenient for you. The cheque is for anything you need. Your van will be along today, and I'll phone you tonight. Yours, James.'

She couldn't credit it. She read it again, and then she turned to Robert Gillian, who seemed to be examining a crystal paperweight that stood on the bureau, and said, 'Do you know what's in here?'

'Ah—yes. My congratulations.' He replaced the paperweight.

'Thank you.' A less reserved girl might have asked, 'Isn't this a crazy business? Does he just expect me to report there at eleven o'clock?' But Louise was too embarrassed to discuss the situation with this disapproving man.

He was disapproving. His expression looked as though congratulations were the last thing he really felt like saying, and she could understand his attitude. He knew Paula. He must think his employer had gone mad, choosing Louise Latham as Paula Cavell's successor.

'Is there any way I can be of service?' he asked stiffly. 'With your business, for instance. You'll be leaving here immediately after the wedding, I hear. If you have any problems——'

Louise did have problems, but they weren't connected with her job, and she said, 'I haven't thought about that yet. If you don't mind, I——' She indicated her housecoat, her general air of having been caught half way through breakfast, and he said hurriedly;

'Of course, of course. This is my phone number.' He put down a small white card. 'James will be ringing you later in the day. If I could have your passport.'

It was in her bureau drawer, all ready for her Spanish trip. She handed it over without a word, and he said, 'Thank you. Good morning, then, Miss Latham, good morning.'

'Good morning,' she echoed. He was out of the door, and she put down the cheque and the letter by the card, and frowned at them as though they were three pieces in a complicated puzzle.

She needed someone to talk to about this. Someone with plenty of common sense, who would advise her and wouldn't gossip. She couldn't sort this out on her own.

Barbara Cole was the obvious choice. From the day Louise first went to work, as a shop assistant for the Coles, right from school, Barbara had spotted her talent and encouraged her. When she had decided to branch out as a designer on her own Barbara and her husband had rented her a room as an office, and the happy friendly relationship had continued.

They sometimes sent customers to her, and she often got her materials through them. They had both been delighted when she was asked by Paula Cavell to do the interior of Tir Glyn.

Barbara was in the shop when Louise walked in and came hurrying to meet her, a slim woman, in scarlet slacks and scarlet silk blouse, hair drawn back in a chignon. 'Hello!' she called, then dropped her voice to ask, 'What's going on?'

Barry had phoned the Coles when he was trying to find Louise. Until then they had thought she was on holiday with him. When Barbara rang him back later he had told them Louise was in Wales, but Barbara was concerned and glad to see her now. Although Louise's 'I must talk to you' wasn't very reassuring.

'Of course, let's go up.'

They went up the stairs into the flat over the shop, and into the little sitting room overlooking the main road. Then Barbara asked, 'Trouble with Barry?'

She was certain that was what Louise wanted to talk about, and when Louise said, 'No,' she gasped. She gasped again, and louder, when Louise went on, 'I met another man this week, and he's asked me to marry him.'

Barbara sat down, but Louise went to the window and looked out at the people and the traffic. After a few seconds Barbara asked, 'What's he like?'

'You're not going to believe this.' She wasn't really looking at anything down there. 'He's loaded. Charm and money.'

'Sounds wonderful,' said Barbara shakily, after another little pause.

'Too wonderful,' said Louise. 'It's James Fenton.'

Barbara knew that Louise was preparing Tir Glyn for Paula Cavell and James Fenton, and she sat there at a loss for words. That didn't happen often. Barbara Cole was a brisk businesswoman in her late thirties. It took a great deal to surprise her, but now she opened her mouth and nothing came out.

Louise left the window and took the other matching armchair and said, 'I've been there just over a week and so has he.' She wouldn't go into all that business about Tom Reading, it was complicated enough without that. 'We—got on well together,' she went on, 'and yesterday he said that he and Paula were through, and he asked me to marry him.'

'He *did*?' Barbara croaked.

Perhaps she would find it easier to believe if Louise explained that it hadn't been a passionate declaration, more of a business offer with a ring thrown in. 'He said he needed a wife and he was tired of cheats and he admired my integrity.'

'How do you feel?' Barbara leaned forward, scanning Louise's face.

'I don't know,' Louise admitted. 'I think I'm scared. We're supposed to be getting married here a fortnight on Wednesday.'

Barbara whistled soundlessly. 'Is he *here*?'

'No, he's gone. I don't think I'll see him till then.' She twisted her hands together. 'And I don't know what to do.'

'Marry him,' Barbara said firmly, her practical nature asserting itself. 'You won't get another chance like this.'

'That's for sure,' murmured Louise wryly.

'So you've caught him on the rebound.' Barbara was beginning to believe it, and beginning to be thrilled. 'But if he feels it's time he got a wife he could do a lot worse for himself.' She and her husband were very fond indeed of Louise. 'You're getting married here?' She was going to ask what sort of arrangements had been made, and offer to help, when Louise said quickly,

'That's what he says, but don't tell anyone, will you? I don't know for sure that it's going to happen, or that I want it to. There's always a chance that he's using me to get back at Paula. If she hears he's thinking of marrying somebody else she might come rushing back.'

That hadn't occurred to Barbara, but a man as successful as James Fenton might use people callously. A girl like Louise might get hurt. It would be a wicked thing to do and she rushed to deny it. 'I think it's more likely he's caught her out, what he said about cheats. And I think he's decided he wants somebody completely different, whom he can trust. And you're a girl he can trust. And there aren't too many of us about these days.'

'You're a cynic,' said Louise, smiling.

'I think he's fallen in love with you,' declared Barbara, who was a romantic at heart, under it all.

No, thought Louise. He has reasons for asking me to marry him. They may be the reasons he gave me or they may not. But love, as you mean it and as I mean it, is not among them.

CHAPTER SIX

THERE were several business letters waiting for Louise in her office, and she was undecided how to deal with those that might mean work. She had no immediate commissions. She had expected to spend her next four months at Tir Glyn, but now she wasn't certain what she would be doing. There might be time on her hands when she would be needing all the work she could get.

She wrote, explaining that she was booked up at the moment, asking if she might get in touch later, and then went back to her flat. There was no sense staying by the office telephone when she couldn't say where she would be in two weeks' time.

She had several calls at home that day. News that she and Barry had broken up had got around. Friends were curious, and Louise obliged, up to a point.

She admitted that it was all off between herself and Barry, and everyone sympathised. They all seemed to take it for granted that it was he who had walked out, and she let them. But she said nothing at all about James Fenton.

He phoned that evening. Barbara had come round. Louise had shown her the letter Robert Gillian had delivered this morning, and the cheque, and Barbara had said that it seemed like a genuine proposal, and what did he look like?

'Dark,' said Louise. 'Striking.' She remembered the unforgettable thin-lipped face and wondered how to describe it. Then she said, 'I don't know. Women eye him even when he's dressed like a scruff. He isn't over-tall, but he seems it. I suppose it's personality. He looks——' she paused, biting her lip, then she said, 'He looks the sort of man Paula Cavell would be seen around with.'

'Yes—well, he was, wasn't he?' said Barbara, and that was when the phone rang.

'Louise?' said James.

'Yes.' Barbara had just read the line in the letter, 'I'll phone you tonight,' and she was sitting very still, trying to read from Louise's expression who this was. 'Sorry I had to dash off this morning. Is the date all right for you?' The only date he had given her was the date on which he proposed they should marry, and Louise stammered,

'Well—yes.'

'Good. I'll be away for the next ten days. You can contact me through Robert if you need to.'

'Oh.' It was all so matter-of-fact that it took the wind out of her sails, but he went crisply on.

'I'd prefer the wedding to be as quiet as possible. Do you mind that? Would you mind postponing the re-ception until we return?'

'No.' She seemed to be responding automatically.

'How are you?' he asked. Louise felt as dazed as she had when she'd raised her head after falling down the steps.

'Fine,' she said.

'The elbow all right?'

'Yes.' She had replaced the dressing and she had several bruises, but her whirling mind had nothing to do with her fall. It was this talk of marrying a man who sounded as though he had jotted down the time and place in his desk diary that was the real shaker.

'Good,' he said. 'I'll be in touch.' And he rang off.

As Louise put down the phone Barbara asked, 'Was it——?'

'Yes, it was.'

Louise had hardly said anything. If that was James Fenton, thought Barbara, he didn't go in for long telephone chats.

Louise came back to the little low white table where the letter and the cheque lay among the tea-cups for two and a box of shortbread biscuits. 'He'd like it to be a quiet wedding,' she said. 'And can we postpone the reception until we get back from a month's sales tour.'

'That's all?' Barbara's neatly arched eyebrows rose high.

'That's all.' Louise took another biscuit.

'Businesslike,' said Barbara.

'Very,' Louise agreed.

She bit on her biscuit and Barbara asked, 'So what are you going to do about things? You don't have much time, even if you are cutting out the reception. You'll have to get a trousseau, and do you have bridesmaids at a register office, or is it just witnesses? And the licence? Will he see about the licence?'

'I don't know,' said Louise, 'but I'm doing nothing. I'm not making any arrangements and I'm not telling anybody but you. I'll be here on the ninth and then we'll see what happens.'

She made a small grimace, laughing at herself and pretending it was funny, although Barbara wasn't fooled. 'A lot of folk remember Douglas Bayley, and now they think that Barry's jilted me. I don't want it getting around that I'm the twice jilted girl who put it about she was going to marry a millionaire, and got turned down for the third time.'

It was a strange fortnight, a sort of limbo. Louise re-papered and painted the little alcoves in the shop for Barbara, to amuse herself and pass the time. When anyone asked why she wasn't in Wales she said there had been a hold-up on that job, and that was true enough.

Barry must have heard she was here, and she was glad he didn't try to contact her. Her friends were mostly his friends too, and they were being tactful and giving her time to get over the break-up before they included her in invitations again.

James phoned three times; each call was friendly, but no more than friendly. And the date still stood, the ninth of the month at eleven o'clock, when her company was requested at a wedding. Her own.

She really did go through those two weeks in a daze so far as Wednesday the ninth went. It seemed a vague and impersonal arrangement, until the last call, when the day was tomorrow and the voice on the phone was telling her, 'I'll call for you at a quarter to eleven.' Then she said,

'You *mean* it.'

'What?'

'We are going through with it?'

'Do you want to back out?' he asked.

She hadn't had much luck with men before, but everyone would say this had to be incredible luck. James Fenton asking her to marry him. She had always been careful before, and no one had loved her for it, so why not take a chance and accept what the fates were offering? A leap in the dark would make a change.

'No, I don't want to back out,' she said.

'Until tomorrow, then. I'll collect you at a quarter to eleven from your apartment.'

'I'll be here.' She heard him replace the phone, and did the same, and knew that she had to snap into action. She had nothing ready, nothing. At the least she had to pack for a month abroad, and the clothes she had were hardly what James Fenton's wife would be expected to wear. If she was going into this she would do it wholeheartedly. She would do her utmost to live up to whatever expectations he had of her.

The clothes she had bought for her holiday with Barry were still in drawers and wardrobe, unworn. They were mostly casual beachwear type, but she went through them all now, selecting a few and putting them on the bed. Then she picked out the best of her basic wardrobe, a blazer jacket flannel suit, a couple of dresses, and looked at the lot and knew that she had to do some shopping.

For one thing, she needed a wedding dress. She couldn't marry James Fenton in any of this. She couldn't imagine what she could marry him in.

She ran back to the phone and dialled for Barbara. 'Will you come shopping with me?' she asked.

'It is on, then?' Barbara had found the waiting period very nerve-racking. She hadn't breathed a word to anyone but her husband, and there had been times when she had longed to phone up Mr James Fenton and ask him if his intentions were serious or if this was some sort of weird joke. For a bridegroom-to-be he wasn't very enthusiastic.

'It seems to be,' said Louise.

She took her own money along on her shopping expedition. She still had that cheque, she hadn't paid it into her bank yet. She had no savings, but there was enough in her current account to buy a few clothes, and she would prefer to provide her own wedding dress. She might be a pauper by his standards, but not quite by her own.

She and Barbara went to an exclusive shop in a nearby town. Neither of them had been inside it before. The windows always looked fabulous, but there were no price labels displayed which was warning enough. Today they went in and at the magic words 'wedding dress' all the elegant assistants smiled.

Barbara swayed slightly when she heard the prices, but Louise was immune to shock today. She tried on dress after dress, and they finally settled for a silky polyester in a small scarlet-on-white pattern, with a mushroom-pleated skirt, and a wide-brimmed fine straw scarlet hat with a silky trim that matched the dress.

As they came out of the shop Barbara said, 'Well, you are marrying a millionaire, aren't you?'

'Didn't you buy a lovely dress when you got married?' Louise teased, and Barbara smiled.

'Of course I did, and I might wear it for the wedding just to show that I can still get into it after fifteen years. Now I suppose we ought to do something about your hair.'

It was silky, straight and floppy, and unless it needed a trim Louise washed and set it herself. She said, 'I think it's too late to start glamorising me. I'm going to be nervous enough. I couldn't take a new personality to live up to.'

She hoped the dress would help, and it would have been a good idea to get professional advice about her hair, but if they went to Barbara's hairdressers several of the staff knew her, and would ask why she needed a last-minute rush appointment. Unless she lied it would get out about the wedding, and she still didn't want the news broadcast.

One certain thing would happen if she didn't keep her secret, there would be publicity. James Fenton marrying a local girl would bring the local reporters to her door, and photographers tomorrow. The London papers would be interested too. That was where the paragraphs about James Fenton and Paula Cavell had appeared, and this would be a gossip column scoop.

He couldn't have told anybody. Nor could Robert Gillian, and if they were keeping quiet Louise felt that something might still happen. The wedding might still be called off.

She stayed with Barbara, and her husband, that night. She would have been a bundle of nerves if she had been left on her own, but she always felt at home in their flat, and she knew that however tomorrow turned out they would support her.

Alan Cole was a mild man, stocky, fair-haired and grey-eyed. Both he and Barbara would have liked the children that hadn't come along, and they looked on Louise as a younger sister. He watched Barbara helping Louise wash her hair and hoped this hush-hush marriage would turn out all right.

Less than a month ago Louise had been hoping to marry Barry Mason and now it was a man who could buy and sell half the town, only nobody had to talk about it. Alan wondered what kind of man James Fenton was and if he didn't turn up tomorrow whether Barbara would feel that Alan ought to do something about it. And what Barbara might feel he ought to do.

Next morning, after a breakfast that neither Louise nor Barbara could eat, they went round to Louise's flat to change into their wedding outfits.

Barbara tried to keep up a cheerful flow of talk, as though neither had a care in the world and this was a marvellous adventure. But in fact she was terribly nervous. It was all too much of a secret she felt, too hole-and-corner.

As the clock crept past half ten Louise became paler and paler. She was frantically dabbing blusher on to her cheekbones, but in spite of it her face looked white with strain, and Barbara thought—if he cares at all about her he should have rung again this morning, or sent somebody or something round. He shouldn't have left her here, waiting to be picked up as though this was an ordinary date for a day's trip. She might have been quite alone for all he knows.

The doorbell rang at twenty to eleven, and it was Alan, who had been told to turn up at that time but who was glared at none the less by Barbara. He gathered by that that the bridegroom hadn't arrived and that she had hoped he was James Fenton, and he began to admire Louise's dress. 'That's a pretty dress, Lou, and your hat's a cracker. I always liked big hats. Do you remember that big hat you had, Barbara? Pink, it was. The one that blew off——'

Barbara took up the tale, with the same desperate gaiety, 'On the pier at Blackpool. It was a lovely hat. I hung over the pier and howled and it went floating away.'

They both laughed merrily and Louise joined in, and Alan produced a half bottle of brandy and said, 'Just a wee dram.'

'Not for me, thank you,' said Louise, but Barbara took the bottle and went to collect glasses from the kitchen. Alan followed her and she whispered,

'It's a good idea, but sherry would have been better. This looks as though we're treating her for shock already!'

She poured a very little brandy into a glass and Alan said, 'That's not going to help much.'

'We don't want to get her tipsy,' hissed Barbara. 'She is supposed to be at the register office in twenty minutes.' She turned a worried face to her husband. 'He will come, won't he? He's not stringing her along for any reason, is he?'

The doorbell rang and she put down both glass and

bottle and clasped her hands together in relief and thankfulness.

Louise would not have been surprised if she had found Robert Gillian outside that door again, with another letter for her. But it was James.

He was wearing a dark grey suit, a beautiful suit. He looked distinguished and elegantly arrogant, and she stood there, silent for a moment. Then she said stupidly, 'It's you.'

'Weren't you expecting me?'

'Yes. Of course.' He came into the room and she turned towards the very slightly open kitchen door, babbling, 'I told you about Mr and Mrs Cole, I used to work for them. They've always helped me. They're my very best friends.'

Alan and Barbara came out of the kitchen, and Louise said, 'Alan and Barbara, this is James.'

They greeted each other with, 'How do you do', shaking hands all round, and Alan said, 'We'll get along, then, shall we? We'll see you at the register office.'

As they got into their car he looked at the gleaming Jensen and said, 'I suppose that's his. Our Lou's done all right.'

'He never kissed her when he came in,' said Barbara with a furrowed brow.

'Well, we were there,' Alan pointed out, and Barbara snorted,

'What difference should that make?'

'Perhaps he was waiting for us to leave.' Alan started up the car and Barbara said darkly,

'Perhaps he was, but he didn't look to me as though he was waiting to grab her. I bet you they're right behind us.'

James didn't take Louise in his arms when Alan and Barbara walked out of the flat. The dress wasn't helping as she had hoped it would. He hadn't looked surprised when he saw her; any small compliment would have helped, but all he said was, 'Shall we go?' and Louise didn't feel beautiful at all.

She was holding her hat and when she put it on her hands were empty. She should have had flowers or something to hold, and she wasn't the type for big hats with floppy brims after all. She nodded, and the hat tilted forward and she settled it firmer on her head and hoped there wouldn't be a breeze blowing.

James held the door open for her. When she locked it she had nowhere to put the keys. He took them, and dropped them into his pocket, then led the way downstairs telling her they would be flying out, first to Paris, then on Sunday to Brussels, and she murmured, 'Yes, I see—yes,' feeling that she should be producing a pad and pencil and taking notes.

As they came out of the house a neighbour, walking along the pavement, said, 'Off to a wedding?' and Louise said again,

'Yes.'

'Lovely day for it,' said the neighbour, who had looked at them admiringly and had no suspicion that Louise might be the bride. They looked exactly like a pair of wedding guests, but they weren't even arm in arm.

Louise got into the car and sat looking straight ahead, and James asked, 'Don't they know you're getting married?'

'No one does but Barbara and Alan,' she said quietly. 'You said you wanted no fuss.'

He looked at her with astonishment. 'You're a very discreet woman. I didn't expect you to keep it a dead secret.'

'Did you tell anyone?' she asked.

'I didn't make any announcements.'

If he had done the press would have been at the register office, but there wasn't a photographer or reporter in sight when they were ushered into a small room where a large jolly-looking man greeted them. He had no idea who James Fenton was, and he married them with only the Coles and Robert Gillian and a woman as onlookers.

Louise made the responses and held out her hand while a ring was slipped on her finger. It was a plain gold band and it would have been awkward if she hadn't been able to get it on—how would they have explained that to the registrar? No one had asked her what her size in rings was.

When she looked at James Fenton standing beside her she knew that she was marrying a stranger, and she wondered who he thought he was marrying. There were all those old films where someone looks at the person they are about to take for better or worse, and sees another face. Then the mist clears and they are back with second best. Louise wondered if James saw Paula Cavell for a moment when he looked at her.

Then the ceremony and the signing were over, and she was in the foyer and Barbara was kissing her, and Robert Gillian was presenting a woman as his wife Lilian.

Mrs Gillian was smiling too, saying she was delighted to meet Louise, and she did hope they would be very, very happy. But her enthusiasm rang false. The Gillians were putting on a good face, but Louise knew that neither of them was happy.

Perhaps they had been fond of Paula. Perhaps they simply thought that James Fenton could have chosen a more suitable wife, and Louise had to agree with them there. He had an arm around her now, but she still felt devoid of every social grace.

She was going to be a dead loss as hostess of Tir Glyn.

She was plain and awkward and she would never learn how to glide and glitter in a hundred years. The only thing she was good at was her job, and what kind of wife did this man think he was going to make of her?

Barbara said suddenly, 'You're not just going off, are you? Won't you all come back home with us and have a drink and some lunch?'

She was reluctant to let Louise go like this. James Fenton was one of the most devastatingly attractive men Barbara had ever seen, but he had a hard face and what might be a cruel mouth, and she knew how sensitive Louise was. Louise was a dreamer, an artist, and Barbara noticed how she held herself rigid within the curve of his arm.

The arm hold wasn't exactly a cuddle either. It seemed more like a hand laid on his property, light and firm. Louise might have married Money with a capital M, but she was not Barbara's idea of a radiant bride. She was smiling as brightly as any of them, but her eyes were bleak.

Impulsively Barbara caught hold of her hand and held it. 'I'm sure Robert and Lilian would be delighted,' said James Fenton, 'but my wife and I have a plane to catch.'

Louise felt herself drawn away, and they all went out into the car park. There was no confetti, no flowers, just a little flurry of shaking hands and being kissed goodbye by Alan and Barbara.

She hadn't been kissed by her husband. The bridegroom was supposed to kiss the bride, wasn't he? Why hadn't he? she wondered.

She waved as the car left them behind, and saw that they had all stopped smiling. They stood there in their wedding finery, four worried incongruous faces.

James gave her a quick grin that should have been reassuring. She had done nicely so far, he seemed to be saying, although she had done nothing except stand around and say the words she was told to say. This was like taking on a very complex task without knowing what was expected of you at all.

'I need a wife,' he had said. And now here she was, with his ring on her finger and a brand new name in her passport. Louise Fenton. It was better than Lilian Gillian. She had probably thought twice before she took on that surname.

To her surprise and horror she felt laughter bubbling in her throat, an insane urge to laugh her head off, to laugh and laugh. This was hysterics—it had to be. Nothing was that funny, especially today. If she started to laugh she would never be able to stop, unless she started to cry, and James would think he'd married a crazy woman.

He was driving her back to her apartment to collect her cases, and she bit her lip until it hurt and clenched her hands tight, and by the time the car drew up the wave of hysteria had subsided.

She hadn't known her nerves were that strained, she had never been hysterical, but she was very, very edgy. If she unclenched her jaws her teeth would start to chatter. She got out of the car and went upstairs, and if anyone had spoken to her it would have taken a tremendous effort to have answered them in anything like her normal voice.

James said very little, and she got away with answering him in murmurs. He opened the door and she said, 'My cases are in the bedroom.'

While he fetched them she went from room to room, into the bathroom, back into the living room, then into the kitchen, as though she was off on a holiday and was doing a quick check that all the lights were turned off.

She didn't really know what she was checking, she

didn't know when she would come back. She had left the second set of keys with Barbara last night. The place would be safe until she knew what her plans were, but she had to keep moving, she couldn't stand still.

In the kitchen Alan's half bottle of brandy stood beside the sink, together with a glass with a little brandy in the bottom, and Louise would have poured herself a drink if she had dared. It might have steadied her, but what could she say if James walked in and caught her?

She took off her scarlet straw hat and dropped it on the table, and dropped down herself in a kitchen chair.

James opened the door and looked at her and asked, 'Are you all right?'

'Don't I look all right?'

It was as though he hadn't noticed before. He went to the sink, swilled out the glass, poured a fresh measure and said, 'Drink this. You look as though you need it.'

Her hands were shaking. They talked about pre-wedding nerves. She had post-wedding nerves because she was realising now, and fully, what a leap in the dark she had taken. She had just assumed the role of Mrs James Fenton with no guarantee that she could fulfil any of the obligations. Especially the first, the most immediate and intimate, tonight.

James Fenton would certainly be an experienced lover, but he might not be a gentle and patient wooer, and she was painfully reserved. She didn't want to be but she was, she always had been, and the naked passion of sex without love would be a terrifying ordeal for her.

She drank the brandy, coughing on it. Then she said, 'Won't you have a drink?'

'No, thank you.'

'You don't need one?'

'No.'

He might at least have raised a token glass and said, 'Here's to us.' It was as though he was deliberately making her feel ill at ease. If he hadn't wanted this marriage why had he gone through with it? He could have called off at any time.

She said, 'You look as though you're regretting it already.'

'Not at all.' His lips curved slowly, but it wasn't a reassuring smile. It was too sardonic and rather scaring. 'I'm sure you'll make exactly the kind of wife I need,' he said. 'And I hope to live up to your requirements.'

'Mine?' She washed the glass under the tap and a little water splashed on her expensive dress. 'What do you know about what I want?'

'Enough,' he said, and she thought—then you know more than I do, because I don't know what I expect or hope from this marriage. Of course the advantages were obvious when a working girl married a very rich man, and perhaps it would be all right. If only tonight were over.

Louise left her hat behind. The outfit looked less dramatic, less bridal without it. They were going straight to the airport and she was more comfortable without a hat. When she wrote to Barbara she would say, 'The hat's a present, to take the place of the one you lost off Blackpool pier. Alan said he liked floppy hats.'

James hadn't said that. He hadn't said he liked anything about her today, although he was talking to her in the car now, like a charming stranger whom she might have met half an hour ago.

Louise listened intently. She answered and she made a few remarks herself, and they reached the airport having discussed the weather, and heard the news bulletin on the radio and talked around it. The rest of the time the radio played.

In the plane anyone who overheard would have been certain they were boss briefing employee. James told her who he was going to meet first in Paris— David Fox, agent and representative of Fenton Structures in France; what he would be doing there— attending a conference on the stress safety structure.

'I'll have to do a little entertaining and I'll expect you to hostess for me, and accompany me on social occasions,' he went on, 'but you'll have plenty of time to shop and see the sights.'

'On my own?'

'Not if you want company. That can be arranged.'

'Not you?'

He smiled. 'I literally don't have any spare time. I wish I had.' He took papers out of his briefcase, and she turned over the pages of one of the magazines she had bought at the airport.

This was a business trip, arranged before he had decided to use it as a honeymoon, but if he had been here with Paula Cavell she suspected that he would have organised himself some spare time.

What was the stress factor? How far you could impose on steel or concrete? A pity it didn't include human beings, because she felt that her own stress safety factor was getting pretty near snapping point.

They were met by a uniformed chauffeur, driving a limousine, and in the hotel foyer by a young man, who sprang eagerly forward when they walked through the revolving doors. He looked every inch a company man, right on the ball. His eyes gleamed, spotting James Fenton, as though this was his big moment.

He thought Louise was a secretary. She hardly got a look until James said, 'This is my wife,' and then, briefly, the gleaming eyes popped. He recovered at once, and welcomed her effusively, then went to the lift with them, assuring them that food would be sent up immediately.

'I'll see you in about an hour,' said James.

The suite was palatial. Louise tried to look at it with a professional eye and she couldn't fault it. Then a trolley of food arrived, and that should have been fun because it looked wonderful. They helped themselves, but James was preoccupied to the exclusion of interest in either the food or her. He ate at a desk, and she sat by the window looking down into a square below.

If David Fox could have seen them now he would have been even more astonished. He must know they were newly married, and with business taking up so much of their honeymoon time he would certainly be expecting them to be very much tête-à-tête over this meal. Instead of worlds apart, hardly exchanging a glance or a word.

When James gathered up his papers, and said he had to go, Louise was quite relieved. After that she felt free to walk around, examining everything. She unpacked and hung up her clothes, then went into the black marble bathroom and bathed and changed.

She would have enjoyed this under different circumstances, but she couldn't relax. 'Back about ten,' he had said, and she watched the clock now with more dread than she had this morning.

If he hadn't turned up this morning no one would have known but Barbara and Alan; and she wished now that he hadn't. If she stayed dressed she might have to undress in front of him. It might be better to get into bed, to read her magazines in bed. She wouldn't look so awkward then.

She looked at herself in the mirror, wearing her long white cotton nightdress, with its demure high neck and frilled cuffs, and knew that she hadn't a scrap of glamour. There were hollows under her cheeks and her mouth was too big. Beneath the nightgown there were collarbones and rib bones, and her breasts were too small.

Every girl in every magazine was more beautiful than she was. Even the ones who weren't glamour girls, the ones who had written the articles on food and music and the world's problems.

I'm a freak, she thought, a great auk. What am I *doing* here? She didn't hear James come into the sitting room, but when he opened the bedroom door she shot up in bed.

'Hello,' he said. 'Still awake?'

Louise had thought of pretending to be asleep, and now she wished she had because he sounded as though he had expected her to be. She couldn't speak and when he came in again from the bathroom, barefoot, wearing a dressing gown and with his hair wet, she was still sitting bolt upright, the magazine open at the same page in front of her.

He looked across, with weary exasperation, and said, 'Relax, for God's sake.'

'Have you had a busy evening?' she asked jerkily.

'Yes, I have had a busy evening,' he said. 'No, I am not tired.'

Her nightdress felt tight at her throat. Beneath the dressing gown he didn't appear to be wearing anything, and he stood there looking at her. 'Why did you marry me?' he asked.

'I—don't know.'

She really didn't know. She had gone into it in a

daze. She didn't know why. The dressing gown was brown, silk and heavy, fastened at the waist with a cord, open to the waist, and dark hair curled on his chest. His dark eyes flickered over her and she knew how she must look. 'I've got money,' he said cynically, 'but I expect my money's worth.'

'I'm sure you do,' she whispered. He took a couple of steps towards her and her eyes went blind with fright, but at the side of the bed he stopped and said, not unkindly,

'Don't worry, the world's full of willing women. I don't need to resort to legalised rape. I need a wife around to stop the willing ones badgering me to marry them, but I don't give a damn if it's a marriage in name only.'

'You don't?' she was still whispering.

'If that's the way you want it, it suits me.' He smiled, thin-lipped. 'You play your part and I'll keep my bargain. I'll get you well established in your career.' She stared at him and he touched her, a very light fingertip trailing down her cheek. 'Just, don't ever consider two-timing me, because I wouldn't like that.' There was menace in him then, that chilled her spine. But he laughed suddenly, starting to undo the cord of his dressing gown. 'And now you'd better close your eyes, because I don't intend to change the habit of a lifetime.'

He was naked beneath the robe. He crossed the room to turn out lights, dark skin and smooth rippling muscles, narrow hips, narrow thighs, and the lights went out.

Louise was in the dark, except for the long oblongs of the windows, and she slid down into bed. She turned the ring on her finger and it was loose, it was a little too large. You could lose a ring like that. Would he call it cheating if she lost her ring?

She heard his bed creak slightly as he settled in it, and his deep regular breathing. She pulled the satin sheets over her head and began to shiver.

CHAPTER SEVEN

LOUISE woke several times in the night, seeing the pale gold oblong of the windows, listening to James' breathing, looking over to where he lay. Each time a feeling of despair threatened to engulf her. It came instinctively and she told herself every time that things were not so bad. She was being used, this was a business arrangement, but it could have been a whole lot worse. She talked herself into calm, then slept again, but each waking brought that deep subconscious sadness.

When she woke in daylight it was the worst of all. James was moving around the room. He was dressed but jacketless, and she closed her eyes again. She didn't want him to realise she was awake, and she repeated to herself her solace of the night, 'It isn't too bad, it could be worse.'

He was putting in cufflinks now, thin gold cufflinks, she had noticed them yesterday, discreet and pricey; slipping on a dark green tie over the pale green shirt and fastening it. She watched him through her lashes and thought it would have been comforting if he had been prepared to spend today with her. Her first day in Paris. The first day of her honeymoon. She wondered what she was supposed to do with today.

There was a tapping on the sitting room door, and James went out of the bedroom. Louise heard the murmur of voices and the sound of wheels being trundled over the carpet, and she sat up.

He was pushing a breakfast trolley, with croissants, butter, marmalade, fruit, and a large coffee pot. 'Ready for breakfast?' he enquired.

'Please. Coffee.'

He knew how she took her coffee—a little milk, a little sugar. He prepared a cup for her, then poured his own, black, and took it into the sitting room. Through the open bedroom door she saw him at the desk with the inevitable briefcase. 'I'll have David Fox and a couple of business colleagues and their wives with me this evening,' he said. 'Do you speak French?'

'Only what I learned at school.' That wasn't going to get her far.

'It doesn't matter.' Did he mean it didn't matter if she couldn't follow the conversation, or that they all spoke English and would adapt themselves to her? 'But be here at six, won't you?' he said.

He came back into the bedroom, finishing his coffee, putting on his jacket, telling her, 'I'll be making you an allowance, of course. In the meantime that should get you through the day.' There was a pigskin wallet on the dressing table. 'Anything you want to buy in the way of clothes Michelle will charge for you.'

'Who will?'

'Michelle Benoit. She works in David's office. She'll be along to show you around.' He put down the cup on the trolley, and that seemed to be all the breakfast he wanted, because he said, 'Have a good day,' and went.

Louise finished her coffee, sipping it slowly, before she got out of bed and went to look at the wallet. She didn't like this at all. She didn't like his attitude of, 'Here's your cash for the day, run along and amuse yourself.' As his wife she might be entitled to an allowance and clothes through a charge account, but it seemed so businesslike that it was sordid.

She might be entitled to it, but she didn't much want it, and when she opened the wallet she looked with distaste at the wad of notes. She wasn't for sale. She would account for what she spent, and this lot would more than last out her stay here.

She bathed and dressed more hurriedly than she would have done if she had been left to her own devices, because she didn't know what time her guide for the day would be arriving. She had intended to wear a matching cream linen dress and jacket that she had bought at the same time as her wedding dress, but she changed her mind and decided on jeans and a blue cotton jersey shirt.

She was a tourist, a sightseer. There was no need to dress up as Mrs James Fenton until six o'clock tonight, when he would expect her to act the hostess for his business colleagues.

She sat at the window, eating hot croissants and watching the teeming life in the square below. She saw a man and a girl by a flower-seller. He was buying flowers and they moved away hand in hand, the girl's head bowed over her posy. It was probably sweet-scented, and Louise sighed, not sure even now how she herself could have walked so tamely into a loveless marriage. Money was a long way from the be-all and end-all of her life, and yet here she was on a honeymoon that offered nothing but material things.

There was a bitter taste in her mouth under the sweet tang of the marmalade, and she tried to work up a little excitement for the day's sightseeing. She *was* in Paris. Then she was off to Brussels and Amsterdam and Hamburg. She would see everything she could, all the marvels there were, and stop calling this a honeymoon because it wasn't. It was a business trip, and she was very lucky to have been taken along.

The phone rang, someone telling her that a Mademoiselle Benoit was here, and she said, 'Thank you, I'll be right down.'

The foyer was large, and there were so many people about that she realised as she stepped out of the lift that she should have asked for a description of Mademoiselle Benoit. She stood, staring helplessly around for a moment, and was just about to make for the reception desk when a young woman came forward.

'*Excusez-moi, madame, mais êtes-vous* Madame Fenton?'

'Er—yes.'

Mademoiselle Benoit was as tall as Louise, with skirt, blouse and single-strap shoes in merging shades of violet; and beret and three bracelets in stinging pink. David Fox had probably told her what Louise looked like, but even so she stared at Louise as though there had to be some explanation, and Louise felt very weary.

This was going to go on. Everyone she met was going to wonder why James Fenton had married her, and one day she just might tell them. This girl, with her soignée assurance and her sharp eyes, made her uncomfortable. She was sure this girl would gossip in her office, about her day with the extraordinary Mrs Fenton.

'So what shall we do?' asked Louise. 'I'm new in town.'

'You have never been to Paris before?' The accent was delightful; Michelle Benoit was astonished. 'But that is not possible!' she said.

'Oh, but it is,' said Louise.

'Perhaps you would like to see the shops?' Michelle Benoit suggested as though something should be done about Louise's appearance.

'Lovely,' said Louise.

It would have been lovely with Barbara, or with

several other friends Louise could have named, but Michelle Benoit was patronising. She didn't mean to let it show. She was shrewd and ambitious and had no intention of getting on the wrong side of the boss's wife. She piled on the charm, nothing was too much trouble, Louise's whim was her command, but she thought Louise was unsophisticated, and compared with Paula Cavell quite painfully plain.

Louise saw that in her expression, her smile, her eyes. She would certainly go back to the office and tell them that the new bride was whatever was the French equivalent of a drag.

She took Louise to the boutiques of the 'name' coutures, and along the Rue du Faubourg St Honoré, the Place Vendôme and the Champs-Elysées, where the shop windows were out of this world. Of course Louise saw things that she coveted: beautiful soft suede suits, high fashion French shoes, but she had no intention of buying anything to wear under Mademoiselle Benoit's hypercritical gaze.

After lunch, back at the hotel, she thanked her and said she had letters to write and hoped to see her again before they left Paris. Mademoiselle Benoit said that anything she needed—and Louise said hastily, 'You've been a great help, thank you very much indeed,' and made her escape up to her empty suite.

It was like escaping from a jailer, or a reporter who was taking a mental note of everything she did and said. She flopped into a chair for a few minutes, closing her eyes and relaxing, then came down into the foyer again. She was going sightseeing on her own. She would have preferred company, but not the patronising kind.

Michelle Benoit was still here, and that stopped Louise in her tracks, although Mademoiselle Benoit was too busy talking to be gazing around. She sat with another woman, laughing, gesticulating, telling what looked like a hilarious tale. 'And no prize for guessing who she's talking about,' thought Louise wryly.

She walked out of the hotel, not much caring if Michelle spotted her or not, and the commissionaire got her a taxi. She went to the Louvre and found the Mona Lisa, and came back in plenty of time for her evening appointment, feeling that it hadn't been a wasted day after all.

There was no sign of James. She bathed and changed into the dress she had worn for her wedding, then sat at her dressing table, taking care with her make-up.

She had seen some beautiful clothes today, some fabulous things—dresses and lingerie out of a dream. One nightdress was surely made for a bride, and she wondered if she dared go back tomorrow and buy it. She really should buy something special while she was in Paris.

She heard James call, 'Hello,' and went to open the bedroom door and say her own, 'Hello'.

'Ten minutes,' he said. 'You look very elegant.'

'Do I? Thank you.'

He went through the bedroom into the bathroom. Louise heard the shower running, and she sat by the window in the chair she had sat in last night and this morning. This was her honeymoon suite, her favourite chair, but he had never sat here with her, and now when he came out of the bedroom it was time to go downstairs.

He was in a lounge suit, and he looked fantastic, he always did. 'Did Michelle show you the sights?' he asked.

'She showed me the shops.'

'What did you buy?'

'Nothing.'

He frowned slightly, as though he had expected her to buy. Of course his wife needed a bigger and better selection of garments than the few things hanging in the wardrobe, and she suspected that Michelle Benoit had been told to get her 'kitted out'. She said, 'I had the impression that Miss Benoit would have taken back a full report on any garment I chose.'

He went on frowning, asking, 'Would that have mattered?'

'I suppose not.'

... 'You can be too sensitive,' he had told her when he was Tom Reading ... 'You can't go on wearing that dress,' he told her now. 'Attractive though it is.'

'Of course not,' she said ironically, 'your wife must do you credit. I'll get something new tomorrow. But I would rather go on my own.'

'Just as you like,' he said. 'Now shall we go down? Our guests are waiting.'

The men were middle-aged, an architect and a contractor, and both looked rich, which meant successful. Pierre Pellerin was fattish, and Jules la Clainche was thinnish. Monsieur Pellerin had a much younger wife, a very beautiful red-haired girl with hungry eyes that rarely left James.

Madame la Clainche was a svelte Parisienne, about the same age as her husband, chic in a low-cut black dress that showed her smooth white shoulders and a splendid emerald necklace.

Louise was introduced, and they all looked so hard at her that the only way she could keep her cool was by pretending they were clients—her clients. She wasn't shy with clients because she knew she was good at her job. If she stood here as Mrs James Fenton then she was conscious of all her failings, but as Louise Latham, interior decorator, she was calm, watching and listening and assessing their style, taste, characters, forgetting herself entirely.

It was a delicious meal: turbot in Bearnaise sauce, duck and orange, asparagus and butter, cheeses and a soufflé flavoured with liqueur.

They talked like old friends, in English for her benefit, and it was funny that she had pretended they were clients, because it seemed they had been told her profession and almost as soon as the meal was under way Fernande la Clainche, the contractor's wife, was asking for advice.

'I have a bedroom with which I am not happy. We have recently moved into this house, you understand —you will see on Saturday.' Will I? thought Louise, nobody told me; but she smiled and listened.

'It is nót a large room, but the ceiling is too high,' Madame continued.

'What colour is the carpet?' Louise asked.

'Green, the green of apples.'

'If you paint the ceiling the same colour it should help get the room into proportion.'

'Ah yes.' They began to discuss optical illusion tricks, and Madame inquired if Louise would be continuing her career now that she had married.

James answered for her. 'My wife is a professional in her own right.' He put a hand over Louise's hand and smiled at her. 'She wouldn't be happy living in anyone else's shadow.'

He sounded as though he admired her for it, and she wondered if he did. She wondered if it was true, but it made her feel more at home at this dinner table, among these successful people. He was telling them that she was a success too.

He did that all evening, supported her. When he looked at her or spoke to her none of the others could have guessed this was a convenience marriage; and she felt her colour rise and her breath quicken when their eyes met.

When they were back in their suite she said, 'I hope I didn't let you down.'

'Let me down?' There was one small side lamp burning. He had crossed the room to draw the curtains and he stood outlined against the window. 'Why should you have let me down?'

'They're all very successful, aren't they? They'd expect your wife to be something special.'

'And aren't you?' He might be laughing at her, she couldn't see his expression clearly, but she was glad he had said that.

She went to stand beside him and look down into the square that was almost deserted now, and she said, 'There's a flower-seller there in daytime. I watched this morning. I'd rather have had a bunch of flowers than that wad of money you left in the wallet.'

'Then you shall have flowers.' He was smiling, his tone was bantering.

'Thank you,' she said. But she didn't want them ordered. She wanted him to buy them for her, better still buy them with her like the young man this morning, taking the posy and giving it to the girl, and then walking off hand in hand with her.

They stood as they had on the terrace at Tir Glyn, but there he had put an arm around her, kissed her. Since she became his wife he had only touched her casually, and yet this evening she had felt or imagined a rapport between them. Almost the way it had been between her and Tom.

'Tomorrow——' she began.

'I'll be away early in the morning and back late, but anything you need——' He was probably going to say 'phone the office' and she said quickly,

'I'll go sightseeing. And I'll buy another dress. Are

'Yes, leaving there Sunday. And if I know them it will be a party.'

'So I'll need something to wear at a party.' She was so conscious of his nearness, and she longed for his touch with an aching hunger.

'And you can look at the bedroom with the high ceiling,' he chuckled, 'but remind her you're a professional. She has a strong streak of thrift, has Fernande, she'll get a free consultation if she can.'

Louise smiled too. 'I can't charge while I'm a guest in their house, can I?'

'Not this time, maybe.' He put an arm around her then, and she rested her head on his shoulder. There was a moon overhead, and down in the square lamplight and moonlight made shadows through the trees.

It was all shadows in the room and she thought—if you would say now, 'I love you,' I don't think that I would be afraid of loving. If you would be gentle and treat me as you did just now downstairs. They thought we were husband and wife, that we would spend tonight in each other's arms.

The phone rang and James went to answer it, turning on more lamps. It was a business call about tomorrow and it lasted a long time. He made notes and talked about things that meant nothing to her. She went into the bathroom and got ready for bed, and when she came out he was still sitting at the desk with sheets of paper in front of him.

'Goodnight,' he called. A few minutes later he came into the bedroom to take a book from a case, and closed the door between them when he went back.

Louise got into bed and he was so long that she wondered if he had gone out again. It wasn't that late, about ten o'clock. He might have gone downstairs or out, and it would have been the easiest thing to find out. She only had to open the door and look, but somehow she didn't want to do that. She didn't really want to know.

She stayed where she was, in bed, and she slept at last. She was tired, she slept soundly, waking as she had yesterday morning when breakfast arrived, and that was all she saw of James until the next night came round.

She enjoyed her day. It wasn't that great a hardship being alone; she had been alone before. She bought a map of Paris and went to some of the places whose names had always intrigued her: the Eiffel Tower, the Tuileries Gardens, Montmartre.

From a smart little boutique in one of the cobbled side streets she bought an outfit for the party—a trouser suit in peach satin, the trousers full, a blouse with a lower neck than she usually wore, and a beautifully tailored jacket. It fitted smoothly, and it took almost all the ready cash she had.

After she had bought it she came back to the hotel for dinner. She had been asked this morning if she would like her meals in her rooms and said yes. If she was dining alone she would rather eat in private. So up it came and she sat there, thoughtfully chewing and swallowing superb food, in a fabulous apartment, with a great bouquet of flowers on a little gilt table in one of the alcoves.

She had flowers all right, but she doubted if James had chosen them. Much more likely he had told someone to get them, probably Michelle Benoit was still in charge of arrangements to keep the new Mrs Fenton happy. It looked like the kind of bouquet she'd select. You daren't even take out a couple of flowers because it was a creation and you'd spoil it. It could have passed for a wreath as easily as for a bouquet.

There had been messages for her at the desk when

she came back to the hotel. She had gone out early. If she hadn't she might have found her day organised. As for her evening, if she wanted to see a show or eat out she was to ring this number.

'No, thank you very much,' she said to the empty room, and dropped the scrap of paper into a small red leather wastepaper basket, embossed with golden fleurs-de-lys.

Although it might have been more sense to have gone out on the town, chaperoned of course. Someone from the company would have gone with her, and it might not have been Michelle Benoit, it might have been someone she found she liked. She liked most people and they might have taken her to the opera, or a night cruise with dinner on the Seine, or to a spectacular club.

She would have been entertained and amused. Instead of which she was sitting around, waiting for James, who wouldn't care whether she was here or not, so long as she wasn't running wild. He wanted a wife on whom there was no breath of scandal, and that was a cheek when he still considered himself free to take on any willing lady he fancied.

If Louise had loved him, if she had had a jealous nature, this would have been a hellish situation. But she didn't and she hadn't, and this was going to be a marriage of friends, to their mutual advantage.

She took a leisurely bath, trying out all the bottles in the bathroom, sniffing each and adding a drop to the water so that she had a mixture of perfumes and colours. It was a daft way to be passing the time, and she would see that she had something to occupy herself if she was going to have a month of evenings alone in hotel suites.

She was in bed when he came. She had left the bedroom door open and she heard him come in and called, 'James?'

... She said James more easily now. Tom was a memory, someone else...

He came into the room and she felt a tingle run up and down her spine, but his smile was the kind of smile he would have given her if she had been fully dressed, sitting on a chair in the sitting room. Seeing her there, in bed, meant nothing much; probably because to him it was nothing new. He was unaffected by the intimacy of the situation.

Louise had never passed a night alone with a man until she got this ring on her finger, but he could walk naked around a bedroom containing a woman without being embarrassed in the slightest degree. She couldn't have done that in front of him, although she was legally his wife. Her inferiority complex would have paralysed her, and she said jerkily, 'I wish I could— have a room of my own. In the—circumstances there isn't any reason why not, is there?'

'No reason at all.' He took off his jacket and hung it in the wardrobe, then his tie, loosening his collar. 'Except that I'd prefer this to look like a conventional marriage, at least for the honeymoon. When we get back home you can have your own room. You'll need an office, you can have a flat with that if you like.'

He sounded brisk and businesslike, and she asked, 'My old office and my old flat?'

'Wherever you like. That's part of the deal.' He smiled briefly. 'That I set up your career in style. And while we're about it there is the matter of your allowance.'

The figure he mentioned made her gulp and he said laconically, 'You'll need it.'

'To be the kind of wife you want?'

'Yes.'

'You really got married so that no one could nag you to marry them?' She went on, because it seemed so contradictory, 'You got yourself lumbered with a wife because you didn't want a wife?'

He was barefooted now, bare-chested, moving around the room with a lithe tread. His back was lean, taut and sinewy, and mahogany brown. Once she had thought that tan came from working, stripped to the waist in the open air. Now she presumed that it was a sun tan because he could go where the sun was whenever he chose. 'That's over-simplifying the situation,' he said.

'I'm a simple soul.'

He had the drawer of the dressing table open and he looked up from it, his eyes meeting hers in the mirror. 'Don't try to fool me,' he said, and her eyes dropped.

He was right, she was a complicated character. Half the time she couldn't understand herself. She smoothed the satin sheet tight over her knees and there was a raw emptiness inside her. 'But wasn't that why you chose me,' she said, 'because I'm a simple soul?'

She shouldn't be probing like this. She was going to bring down danger on herself, and when he turned to face her she shrank a little further back into her piled up pillows.

He spoke quietly, with biting incisiveness. 'I chose you because I don't want a wife who might have too much influence over me. I don't want to be in any woman's power.'

It was hard to believe, looking at that hard face, but he must have been vulnerable once and he was determined it should never happen again. He must have been hurt, and it must have been Paula.

'You don't want to love anyone?' she said, and he

grinned suddenly, looking cynical and devastatingly attractive.

'On the contrary,' he drawled. 'So long as it's strictly physical.'

That wasn't love. Sex with no involvement of the spirit wasn't love. He had married her because he felt nothing for her but liking and trust. Her integrity had been her chief charm. She couldn't harm him, and he was prepared to pay handsomely for this insurance against hurt.

It was a deal between them, a business partnership, but she must guard against getting hurt herself. What he had just said had hurt her, although it was no more than he'd said on their wedding night, and it was her own fault for persisting in the same question, 'Why did you marry me?' She had to say something else, something impersonal, and she remembered her day's shopping.

She said, 'I bought a suit today. It's in there.'

He slid the panel of her wardrobe aside, and the new trouser suit was a little apart from the rest. When he took it out on its hanger it hung limp and shapeless. 'This?' he asked. 'Day or night wear?'

'Day wear, I think. I hope.' She giggled a little, from nervous reaction, that had just been a tense little scene. 'I got it to wear tomorrow night, if there's a party. It's got more shape when I'm in it.'

'I should hope so,' he said, and Louise thought how Paula would have looked, did look. Any occasion to which he took Paula Cavell must have become brighter and more joyful after she'd arrived because she was so beautiful and so famous. She bit on her thumbnail and said,

'Perhaps not all that much more shape,' and he burst out laughing, holding the hanger at arm's length and surveying it quizzically, and she laughed too ...

They were leaving Paris during the afternoon to drive down to the la Clainches' home, and during the morning Louise had her hair styled and set in the hotel beauty salon.

She had worn it in this style for a long time, with a side parting, falling forward over her cheek. It was a hair style you could hide behind, but today when she began to explain how she wanted it set she decided to try taking it back, still smooth but off her face. Her hazel eyes were one of her best features, and the hairdresser was a very skilful young man and this was the most expensive salon she had ever entered.

The result was good. She went back to her suite and took another look at herself in every mirror there was. It was a tremendous tonic, better than her wedding dress or the slinky suit she had bought for tonight.

She was turning slowly, in the centre of the sitting room, like a model, smiling and almost hugging herself, and then blushing as James walked in.

'Hello,' he said.

'I had my hair done.' She grinned sheepishly. 'I was admiring myself.'

He nodded smiling approval. 'A present for you,' he said, and took three boxes in navy leather, one long and flat, one small and square, one larger and square, from his briefcase.

They were obviously jewellery cases. Louise had never gone in for jewellery, except for a wrist watch. No one had ever bought her anything of real value. She opened the large square box, holding her breath and releasing it in a long-drawn-out sigh. 'Oh ...!'

It was a slim gold bracelet, a golden coil; and there was a fine chain to wear round her neck with a circle of white jade inset with gold, engraved with tiny Chinese symbols. And a small pair of gold ear studs.

She said, 'I don't have my ears pierced, I'll get them pierced.'

'They're clip earrings.'

So they were when she took them out of the box. 'I could lose them,' she said. 'I'll be terrified of losing them.'

James was smiling at her. 'It won't matter if you do.'

'But it will. I never had a present like this before. I can wear them with my shapeless suit.' They would be perfect. He had probably told someone else to buy them, as he had ordered the flowers, but she wouldn't let herself think about that, and she glowed with delight.

'You don't wear much jewellery, do you?' he said.

'No, but these are my style.' She slipped the bracelet on her wrist. 'These are what I would have bought if I'd ever had any money left over.'

He grinned. 'Don't tell me times were that hard. You were doing all right, weren't you?'

'In my job? Oh yes.' She went to the mirror to clip on the earrings. There had been no money left because she had handed it over to Barry, but she didn't feel like admitting she had been so gullible, and she said, 'I'm still a beginner, Tir Glyn was my big chance, I had to count the pennies.'

'Well, you won't need to now.'

That was fine, but it took away some of her pleasure, reminding her that these gifts didn't mean much to him. He was rich. They were equivalent to a box of chocolates from most men, and she said, 'That's nice. They're beautiful. Thank you, I shall enjoy wearing them.'

The residence of Jules la Clainche and Fernande his wife was about an hour's run out of Paris, a spectacular place built on a hillside. It was smaller than Tir Glyn but spacious and impressive, overlooking a town of grey roofs, and a winding river edged with yellow poplars.

James and Louise were welcomed warmly, and he was right, there were friends coming tonight, it was going to be a party.

Louise put on her suit and her jewellery. The hairdresser had given her hair a darkening rinse which deepened the red and might have made her pale skin look even more drained of colour. But instead the contrast was almost dramatic. Her skin seemed top-of-the-milk creamy, and the slinky peach of her satin suit took on sensuous lines. The gold, on her wrist, throat and ears, was the final touch she needed, and she came out of the bathroom to James, who had been sitting in their bedroom reading a business report for the last half hour.

'How do I look?' she asked, hopeful but still unsure enough of herself to be dashed by a wrong word or look.

'Stunning,' he said.

So did he, in a dark red velvet jacket, black trousers and a fine lawn shirt. He got up and she wanted him to kiss her, so badly that she knew he mustn't. If he did she would be that much closer to a lifetime of heartbreak. This marriage was playing with fire for her, but it would be her own doing if she got herself burnt.

She said, 'Shall we go down? Is it time to go down?'

'High time,' he said.

After the party they would come back to this room, of course, and that was going to be a difficult situation, because the only bed in here was a double bed. Neither had said a word about that, but it was in Louise's thoughts as she tried her hardest to play her part as James Fenton's new bride.

She knew she was an object of curiosity, and there was an embarrassing moment with a woman who had only just heard the news and came dashing over to embrace James and to look around, demanding, 'And where is darling Paula?'

But on the whole it wasn't too bad. She had given Madame la Clainche so much advice about the decor of her 'awkward' bedroom that that lady went around presenting her to the guests as 'Such a clever young girl.' It was harder to check at a glance for brains than for beauty, so Louise was probably getting intellectual credit she didn't rate. She was smart enough, but she was no mental giant, and she wondered why someone didn't say, 'If she's so clever how come she can't speak French?'

Most of the men were in businesses that were allied to James' business, and much of their talk centred on work. This evening wasn't entirely for pleasure, and Louise watched James, seeing his charm in action, his sure touch and instinctive way of handling each situation. Even when he wasn't speaking English that was easy enough to follow.

'You must be very proud of him,' she was told more than once, and she said,

'Yes, I am,' and wondered if she looked like a dewy-eyed bride.

They went up to their room late, and James sat with more papers while she went into the bathroom, doing all her undressing in there, even to taking off her jewellery. She stripped the make-up from her face and brushed her hair—in its new line, not its old—and got into another of the nightdresses she had brought with her. This one was a pink nylon, sleeveless but still high-necked. She hadn't bought the glamorous nightdress in Paris after all.

She hung her suit in the wardrobe, and put her

jewellery in its box, and then got into bed. It was a big bed, but she would be sharing it with the man to whom she was married and whom she was finding increasingly and dangerously attractive.

She must *not* fall in love with him. That was not part of the bargain. He didn't want that. All she would get for that would be more pain than she could endure.

She lay stiffly, far over on her own side of the bed. If she pretended to be asleep he probably wouldn't touch her or speak to her, but as he got in beside her he said, 'Sorry about this, but the French are a practical race and we are on honeymoon.'

'That's perfectly all right,' she said, and thought how stilted and stupid she sounded. James must have thought so too, because he laughed and said,

'You'll just have to take my word for it that I've never taken a woman by force yet.'

She wished that he would reach out and wrap his arms around her, and hold her close against his warm strong body, and make her laugh and cry, and make her human and loving. But he wouldn't. He wasn't going to give another woman any power over him, after Paula.

She said quietly, 'No, I can't see you losing your head. Especially over me.'

'Do you want me to make love to you?'

He was raised on one elbow, facing her. She turned her head slowly on the pillow, and saw how dark his skin looked against the sheets in the moonlight, and she yearned to touch his skin.

If she did touch him, if she said, 'Yes,' then she would be his wife not just in name; but it would make no difference to the way he felt about her. That was a cold-blooded offer one of the perks of the job of being Mrs James Fenton. No love, but lovemaking if requested, so she said, 'No, thank you,' between gritted teeth.

'You might find it quite pleasant.'

He wasn't offended, he wasn't bothered, he was still smiling at her, and she said tartly, 'You don't get many complaints?'

'Not many.'

'I'm sure you don't.' Then slowly she smiled too. 'I wasn't too bad tonight,' she said, 'I wasn't as tongue-tied as I thought I was going to be. Who shall I be meeting tomorrow?'

He began to tell her. That was their pillow talk, the business trip ahead: Brussels, then Amsterdam, then Hamburg, where he would be seeing his agents, being briefed on operation and growth, meeting customers. Louise would be meeting customers, colleagues and wives, and there was no reason why she shouldn't enjoy meeting them.

She relaxed as she listened, and when he said, 'We'd better get to sleep,' she agreed, but she didn't fall asleep right away. It was a sultry hot night and she was very conscious of James lying a hand's reach away. If she slept she might move without knowing and end up against him, and that kept her huddled on the edge of the bed for a while. But she was tired and at last she drifted off.

She woke to the sound of a far-off rumble of thunder, and instinctively jack-knifed into a sitting position that jerked the sheets and had James instantly awake, asking, 'What is it?'

'Is that thunder?'

He listened. It was very faint. 'Yes,' he said. 'Why?'

Her shoulders were hunched. She had her hands clasped and pressed to her mouth. 'I've got this thing about thunderstorms at night,' she mumbled.

'Rows and thunderstorms at night?' he said.

'Y—yes.'

'Why?' They were nightmare dreads, both of them, a terror that stretched back farther than she could remember.

'I don't know,' she whispered.

There was silence for a moment or two. If there was a storm it didn't seem to be coming closer. An owl hooted in the stillness and James said, 'Well, if you hear it again wake me and I'll think of something to take your mind off it.'

She almost giggled at that. He lay down and seemed to go straight back to sleep, and after listening for a little longer she lay down too. If the storm should come she would wake him, she would have to, but it didn't, and soon she was asleep.

CHAPTER EIGHT

By the end of that sales tour Louise knew why James Fenton was a millionaire. She had watched him at work, seen the incredible pressure that never seemed to tire him. He thrived on it. He rode the crest of the wave with the zest of a winner.

The only time she was alone with him was in their bedroom suites, and often he was still working when she fell asleep.

She worked herself. She played the role of Mrs James Fenton, and when she was dressed and groomed for the part she hoped that she was managing to carry it off. There were fewer popping eyes by the end of the tour. The folk to whom she was introduced as James' bride didn't seem as staggered as Robert Gillian, David Fox and Michelle Benoit had been when they first set eyes on her. So either her appearance was improving, or the initial shock was over for everybody.

She bought more clothes, including some exquisite lingerie because it gave her confidence although no one saw it. Well, James saw it, but he didn't seem to notice. In public he behaved like a husband. In private he was kindly, tolerant, amusing, occasionally abrasive, and apparently quite content to sleep alone.

At any rate he never slept with her. She wondered if he found sex; he'd certainly be offered the opportunity, but his schedule these four weeks was so full that he probably didn't have the spare time. When they got back to England then, of course, but probably not now.

Louise never considered that this might be wishful thinking on her part, because she couldn't bear to believe there were other women, even though this honeymoon was only a business trip.

She told herself she had accepted her strange marriage, with its obvious advantages for her. She was getting a very generous allowance, she had the status of being the wife of a formidably successful man, and she would be flying back to become the mistress of the house of her dreams.

It might not last. James might decide some time that he didn't want this kind of marriage, that he would rather have married Paula after all; but she would still be left with her work. He had promised to help her there, and she filled notebooks with copious details of rooms, decors, materials, and inspirations and ideas that were triggered off on her travels. These four weeks were proving a crash course for her career, as well as giving her the touch of glamour that beautiful clothes and money provide.

But she was glad when the time came to go home. She wanted to get back to work, and she wanted a bedroom of her own. She had never been quite at ease with James in her bedroom, even though he didn't want her, and hardly saw her as a woman. His nearness, especially at night when the world was dark and silent, made her restless. She had been tired most nights, she had slept, but in the morning she had always been glad that she couldn't remember her dreams...

They came to Tir Glyn by helicopter with James at the controls. Louise had done more flying this last month than she had expected to do in a lifetime, but the helicopter was a world apart from the huge impersonal cushioned luxury of the airliners. It was like being in a little car, and she loved it. She followed the map of towns and roads and hills and valleys below, thrilled as a child at a circus; and as they came nearer Tir Glyn she had to hold down an almost painful joy.

She was probably amusing James, but she didn't care. She held her breath as they came down, and when they settled on the lawn and she looked around there were tears in her eyes.

She gasped, 'Isn't it beautiful? The gardens—oh, *look*!' Then she laughed at herself. 'I must be crazy, telling you to look. You knew, of course.'

There must have been feverish activity here while they were away. The lawns were smooth, the borders had the neat professional edging. Bushes had been pruned, laurels cut back, the tangle cleared. Roses grew free of weeds and blooming profusely.

It hadn't lost the wildness that was part of its charm and character, but the borders were filled with flowers that were going to be a blaze of colour. This was how she had imagined it, how he had told her it was going to be. She said shakily, 'Tom has been busy.'

James was helping her down, and for a fleeting moment she thought of Tom and missed him. James said, 'I hope you'll be as happy with the inside of the house.'

'What do you mean?' She knew as they went towards it, and she saw the curtains at the windows. Not all the windows, but it had to mean that some of the rooms were ready to be lived in, and she began to hurry.

There was no moss left on the steps, the wrought iron bench on the terrace was freshly painted, and the front door of the house was open. A woman stood there, wearing a grey linen dress and with soft grey hair and a pleasant face. James smiled and raised a hand in greeting before they reached her. When they did he said, 'This is Mrs Horabin who's going to help us run this place.'

'How do you do,' said Louise, but it was the hall that took her breath away. It shouldn't have done. She had known it would look like this sometime, when the floor had been sanded and polished and the dust and grime had been stripped from the carved staircase and the panelled walls. But everything was mellow and welcoming, and there were beautiful rugs, and beautiful paintings on the walls.

Through open doors she saw the drawing room and the dining room, both looking as though there had never been a time when they had been empty and echoing. There wasn't even a smell of newness, although all the paint and the wallpapers were new. The scent was of roses, there were bowls of flowers around, and the beeswax perfume of old cherished furniture.

She thought—if all this belongs to James, Paula had nothing to bring here. She expected to share this with him, and now I am sharing; and she felt sorry for Paula and a little afraid for herself. She said, 'I feel as if I'm stepping into the past. Or the future. This isn't the house I left behind six weeks ago.'

'There are still some unfinished rooms.' She was glad about that, she wanted to do some more of the work herself, although her designs had been followed to the letter. This was the house she had planned. 'I want to use it right away,' James was saying. 'And now we can. I've disposed of my other house.'

So she would never see where he had lived before he came here. There was a house where he was born in Buckinghamshire, he had told her it was on the market. This was the first she had heard of it being sold, although he had said they were coming back here.

Mrs Horabin said, 'Shall Jack take your cases up, sir?' and a middle-aged man who was standing beside her and looked as though he might be a gardener stepped forward, exchanging broad smiles with James.

'We haven't decided yet which rooms we shall be using.' James put a hand under Louise's elbow. 'Come on, you can make your choice.'

She went upstairs with him, and as soon as they were out of earshot she said, 'Anywhere will do for me. So long as it's my own room.'

'Don't be absurd,' he said curtly. 'You're my wife. You'll obviously have one of the main rooms, preferably next door to mine.'

She shrugged. 'All right.'

She had finished decorating the master bedroom before she left, and now the curtains and the carpets and the great canopied bed were here, it looked as it had been planned to look, like a film star room. This was to have been Paula's, shared with James, and Louise shrank from entering it. She shook her head, but James didn't seem to notice her.

He hesitated a moment in the doorway and then walked in, and as she stood in the corridor she smelt the perfume and knew who had been here. Louise had presumed it was made specially for Paula because she had never come across it anywhere else. It was floral and sweet, but with an underlying sharpness that summed up Paula Cavell.

It lingered on the air in this room as though she had only just left it, or as though she was still here, in the dressing room maybe.

James crossed to the dressing room and Louise had to follow him. Although if Paula was in there she would turn and run. If she could run. If her legs would carry her.

The dressing room was empty. All the fitted furniture was in place, and after the feminine bedroom it looked austerely masculine. There was no one in it, but the scent lingered here too, and propped up on top of the dressing table that ran along one wall was a large photograph of Paula.

She was smiling and radiant, and standing behind James Louise read the message, 'Welcome home, darling,' written in a bold hand across the bottom right-hand corner.

There was no mirror here to show her James' expression. He had his back to her and he said nothing. He just stood there, looking at the smiling enchanting face, and she heard herself say shrilly, 'It seems that Paula doesn't believe it's all over between you and there's nothing more to be said.'

Still he didn't speak. He gave no sign of having heard her and she went on, 'But of course it doesn't have to be, does it? That's the kind of marriage this is. You still have your choice of willing women, but I mustn't cheat. Now that doesn't seem to me to be quite fair.'

'Neither of us will cheat,' he said. 'You're entitled to please yourself what you do, but I want to know. I don't object to you having a love life, but I would strongly object to somebody else telling me about it.'

'Right,' she said. She didn't want to know about his affairs. She didn't want anyone telling her anything. He went past her, out of the room.

There was a phone in this bedroom now, and one in the hall, but she followed him to the top of the stairs and watched as he went down into the study closing the door. In there, in private, he phoned Paula, she was sure of it. He must know where Paula was, and she wasn't far away because it wasn't that long ago since she was here.

Louise was not jealous. If she had been wouldn't she have gone back and torn up that portrait, instead of deciding quite calmly which room she should have?

She walked a little way along the corridor and opened a door, and stepped in and closed the door. The room was ready, freshly painted, very cool in pale peppermint and white. She had liked this room when she was designing it. The furniture was white too and there was a good sized single bed. She would like to sleep in here, she was glad it was one of the completed rooms.

She stood, looking around her, arms crossed and gripping her elbows, in what was a characteristic stance for her in times of stress, although she didn't know it.

She was tired, she told herself. It had been a whirl of a month, and the weather was hot. There was thunder in the air, and thunder always gave her that feeling of black loneliness, as though she was in a hole in space and no one would ever reach to pluck her out.

It was surprising how well she adapted to being Mrs James Fenton during those hot summer weeks. It was an easy life, compared to the life she had lived before. James' success brushed off on her, and after the ordeal of the early days when his friends here were meeting her for the first time and gossip writers were trying to get quotes out of her, there was plenty in life that was enjoyable.

Louise plunged back into her task of completing the house. The army of painters and decorators that must have descended on Tir Glyn for six weeks had disappeared. If she had wanted assistants she could have had them, but she didn't just yet. She would have to start delegating if she wanted to be a name in her own right. Louise Latham, the name she was born with, the name she still worked under, and the name she would be left with one of these days, she had no doubt.

She would have to take on staff if she planned to expand, and she compromised on that when she went back to her old home town for a week and reopened her office there. She did a brisk week's advisory business, and Barbara and Alan's staff handled the practical side.

James was as good as his word in every way. He was prepared to promote her, his firm had a highly efficient public relations department, but she found that Tir Glyn was bringing in her future commissions. The house was a show place, just as she had hoped it would be, to the people who visited it. Often those who had no need of an interior decorator themselves recommended her to others. She had curio value as well, she was the working girl James Fenton had met and married within three weeks, a room designed by her would always be a talking point. But, now she was getting the breaks, hard work and talent could carry her into the big time. Professionally her future looked rosy.

James was here about half the time, and when he was the house was usually filled with guests. The wedding reception had never materialised, but instead Tir

Glyn was an open house to Louise's friends too, to any-one she chose to ask.

While she was on honeymoon she had written to her friends. Most of them had spotted the news of the wedding in the newspapers, but she wrote explaining how sudden it had all been, apologising for not having asked them to the wedding. They all forgave her, they were all thrilled, and there had been wedding presents waiting at Tir Glyn.

Several friends came down in the first few weeks, including Barbara and Alan for a long weekend. Like everybody they were enchanted by the house, and happy for Louise. Alan's delight was unalloyed, but Barbara had slight reservations. Louise seemed to have everything going for her as a happy bride, but Barbara was rather concerned about those separate bedrooms. If you had nine bedrooms you had space to spread aound, but you would have thought that a couple who had only been married a matter of weeks would have wanted to be together at nights.

'Wouldn't you think that?' Barbara asked Alan, as they strolled through the gardens on their first evening at Tir Glyn.

'Perhaps it's the fashion in these circles,' said Alan amiably. Barbara thought, if it was, it was unfortunate for Louise. She remembered that Louise had told her the marriage was an arrangement rather than a love affair, and although Louise was looking very attractive James Fenton had a tremendous sexual charisma. The last man who need spend his nights alone. If Louise wasn't with him Barbara felt that she was making a big mistake.

'It's not a fashion I'd fancy,' she said, and Alan put his arm around his wife's waist.

'Nor me, love,' he said fondly.

Barbara had no idea just how platonic this marriage

was, but Louise felt that there were people who knew. She wondered if the Gillians did. They were often here, Robert was supervising the final stages of the new factory that would be opening about twenty miles away at the end of October, and Tir Glyn had become a second home to them.

It gave Louise no trouble. The house ran like clockwork. The housekeeper presented her with menus and consulted her on household matters, but Mrs Horabin always knew best. She had been James' housekeeper for ten years. Before his father's death she had been his housekeeper. Twenty-five years in the same house, so that she knew James' friends, his tastes and his ways, much better than Louise did. Louise just agreed with everything she suggested.

All the staff, except the local 'daily', had come from James' old home, and Louise was very conscious of the fact that they had known Paula and must be making comparisons. They were all obliging, helpful, but none of them lingered to talk. They did their work and they kept their distance.

Mrs Horabin probably called the tune. Louise would have liked to talk to her and ask her about James, to have heard some of the stories of him as a boy, what his father was like, and the mother who had died when he was born. But Mrs Horabin was always quietly efficient, and Louise was too sensitive to risk a rebuff by showing what the housekeeper might consider too much familiarity.

The couple she liked best in her new surroundings were the Gillians. Robert was nowhere near as pompous as he had seemed at first sight. In fact he wasn't pompous at all. He was a serious-minded man with a saving sense of humour, completely loyal to James and highly intelligent; and Lilian spent hours doing beautiful embroidery and chattering while Louise worked at her decorating.

Lilian Gillian was a large blonde smiling lovely lady, and Louise was glad that the Gillians were so often at Tir Glyn.

She was almost sure they didn't know all the facts about her marriage. Lilian had laughed, describing to Louise what a shock she and Robert had had when James announced that he was marrying and that he wanted no publicity and no fuss, and only Robert and Lilian, as witnesses, at the wedding. She took it for granted now that James and Louise were getting along nicely together, and so they were.

James treated Louise very well. He was very generous. As well as her allowance and charge accounts he brought her presents. She had quite a collection of jewellery to go with those first golden gifts, which she wore when she acted as hostess, or when he took her around with him.

He did that. She was his wife, by title and treatment, except that he never stepped inside the room she had chosen for her bedroom. Several times they had stayed in other houses, but there had always been separate beds and she had always slept alone.

When he was away from home she had no idea where he slept. She knew where he was supposed to be, and those nights she always found it harder to sleep. She didn't know why, she wouldn't let herself make an issue of it. She always blamed it on having worked too late, or a touch of indigestion, anything rather than admit that she hated the thought that James was with someone else so much that she could lie rigid and wakeful half the night.

He didn't tell her. He would have done if she had asked, but she never did, and so far no one else had either. He was probably being discreet, perhaps it

would be a long time before it became general knowledge that James still kept up his bachelor life-style.
When they all knew they wouldn't be surprised, but it
wouldn't be pleasant.

Louise hoped that she wouldn't mind too much when
it happened. And then one evening, six weeks after
their return here, ten weeks after their marriage, Paula
walked in.

James was home and there were visitors—the Gillians
and three others, a TV producer and his wife, who was
an actress. Not as famous or as beautiful an actress as
Paula, but still a face that was recognised when she
walked along the street. The third man owned an airline, and all three had known James for a long time.

It was a beautiful evening, and Mrs Horabin had
just served a delicious meal. They were still sitting at
the dining room table, with the long windows open on
to the terrace, discussing a play that Helga hoped to be
appearing in.

She was telling them about it, making it all very
dramatic, playing her part for them. It had been on
television recently, it was a new play, and both Helga
and Ben her husband thought it might transfer well to
the theatre and a live audience.

Louise was listening, fascinated by this private per-
formance right here at her dinner table, when she
looked across and saw Paula framed in the French
window.

There had been no sound of a car. Voices might
have drowned the footsteps on the terrace, but for a
second it seemed to Louise that Paula had materialised out of thin air. She gave a convulsive start, send-
ing her tiny cup of Turkish coffee spinning across the
tablecloth, and Paula stepped into the room.

She wore her fair hair taken back, like Alice in

Wonderland, and a white muslin dress, sprigged with lavender. She looked like a Victorian child ghost, although she was several years older than Louise, and Louise could only stare, speechless, the colour ebbing from her cheeks.,

Paula came round the table, her eyes dancing, her soft skirts swaying. 'Don't be scared,' she said. 'I'm flesh and blood.' She smiled across at James. 'Aren't I, James?'

'Very much so,' he said. He was smoking a cigar, and it was steady between his fingers. He smiled with a gleam of white teeth; then he stood up, not as though this was in any way an intrusion, as though he was rising to welcome her.

Helga and Ben, and Rex the man who owned the airline, were all smiling, with pleasurable anticipation. Nobody knew what had happened to cause the rift between James and Paula, but they all knew that James had married an unknown without a word to anybody, and at the very least this should spice up the evening.

Only the Gillians were worried. Louise felt as though she had become extra aware, so that no detail of the scene could escape her, and she sensed concern from the Gillians but from nobody else.

Not from James. He didn't mind Paula walking into his home. He wasn't shocked nor surprised. He was cool and amiable, as though she was an expected visitor.

She put out one of her pretty hands towards him. 'Do sit down, don't let me disturb you. This looks so cosy.' Her glance flickered over the dining table, and then over the room, and she nodded, smiling and satisfied. 'Just how I imagined it.' She cast a sidewards mischievous glance at Louise. 'Well, not quite how I imagined it,' and they all smiled with her. Except the Gillians.

She didn't sound bitter, more as though it was a joke—a joke on her, perhaps, but still funny. 'I'd love some coffee,' she said. 'If there's a spare cup.'

Rex brought her a chair and Louise reached shakily for the coffee pot. 'Let me,' said Paula sweetly, 'you're going to spill it.' She looked at the stain from Louise's knocked-over cup. 'Although that wouldn't matter much, would it?'

Paula took the pot and poured herself half a cupful, and Helga asked, 'How *did* you get here?'

'My secretary dropped me at the gates.' She added casually, 'I'm a neighbour. I have this dear little cottage overlooking the sea.'

They were all surprised to hear that, except James. Louise knew that James had known.

'I like it round here,' Paula went blithely on. 'I'd planned to come and live here, as you know. My cottage isn't quite the house I'd expected, but it does. For now.'

Louise had heard news of Paula since she came to Tir Glyn. She had read paragraphs about her. She read the gossip pages now that she was meeting some of the people who were written about, and she knew that Paula's trip to America was over and that she was appearing next month at a drama festival.

People Louise had met since her marriage often mentioned Paula to her, watching for her reaction, but none of them had known about this cottage. Nor that Paula had called at Tir Glyn the day Louise and James Fenton returned.

Some of the staff must have seen her. They might have mentioned her visit to James, but none of them had ever spoken of Paula to Louise.

Well, she was here now, living only a mile or two

away, pouring coffee from the silver coffee pot she had used before, in the room that had been designed for her.

She said, 'The house must be nearly finished. May I see around?' and Louise half scrambled to her feet.

'Not yet. Later.' Paula was using the tone she had used when Louise was working under her orders. She looked around the dining room again. 'But isn't this something?' and her eyes rested once more on Louise. 'Although I'm not saying there haven't been times when I've wished I'd employed another interior decorator. Who *would* have thought it?'

Who would have thought James would marry you, she meant; and she spoke gaily, her lips curved in a smile of pure malice, as though she knew why he had, the background of this marriage, and that James had never once made love to the woman he called his wife.

Louise's face flamed and Paula laughed. 'There, there, I forgive you. Now,' she looked around the table, 'everybody's news, please. I haven't seen any of you for ages.'

Her glance at James was conspiratorial, and Louise felt that no one could miss it. Paula meant them to notice, and to realise that she didn't need to hear James' news, because she had heard it all, and from James.

She was the hostess at that table. It was as though they had been waiting for her, and now the company was complete. Louise sat silent while they talked about mutual acquaintances, and discussed things which were unfamiliar to her. Nobody was bothering to include her any more. She had felt relaxed and content, but now she was the outsider.

Whatever had caused the quarrel between James and Paula they were friends again now. Quite reconciled. Paula leaned towards him, although her chair

had been set with Louise and Rex between her and
James, and Louise felt herself shrinking back in her
chair, staring down at the coffee stain on the tablecloth.

They must all come to her cottage tomorrow, said
Paula. The swimming was fantastic from her cove.

Her huge baby blue eyes were talking to James all
the time. 'You know that, don't you?' they were saying
now. 'You know my cottage and how exciting the
swimming can be from my cove.'

Louise felt that Paula might as well have spoken
these messages, jokes, whatever they were supposed to
be. As an actress she could get her thoughts across with
an expression or a slight gesture, and loud and clear
with those spectacular eyes.

She wished fiercely that Paula would stop playing
this game of secret lovers, and she said suddenly, 'I
think I'd better get this tablecloth soaked before the
stain sets.' She got up and began to take the coffee
things off the table, putting them on the sideboard,
and Paula said,

'Shall we take the drinks into the drawing room, or
on to the terrace as it's such a lovely evening?'

Paula was the natural hostess, just as Louise, frantically clearing the table and dragging the tablecloth
off for washing, seemed to be the obvious one to go
along to the laundry room and get the stain out of the
damask.

Lilian followed Louise, falling into step with her
just outside the door, looking worried and sounding it.
'My dear, what are you going to do about going down
to Paula's cottage tomorrow? I'm not at all sure it's a
good idea.'

She sounded like Barbara. She didn't look like Barbara, but she sounded like her, and it was nice that
somebody cared although nobody could help.

'What can I do about it?' Louise asked, because no one was going to ask her permission, and Lilian accepted that, changing her tactics.

'Well, if we do go I shouldn't let Paula spend too much time with James if I were you. I certainly shouldn't let her get him on her own.'

Louise smiled wryly, imagining herself trying to out-glamorise and out-manoeuvre Paula. She stood as much chance as swimming the Channel.

'Because,' continued Lilian severely, 'she's making it painfully obvious that she hasn't given up. It's too bad of her, buying a cottage here, it isn't giving your marriage a chance.'

So the Gillians didn't know this was a marriage in name only, and that Louise's only rights were financial. She had been endowed with worldly goods, but nothing else. If James wanted to become Paula's lover again he would tolerate no interference from Louise. They were almost certainly lovers now.

She said, 'I trust James.' Lilian might put her down as stupid and blind, but she would expect her to say that, and Lilian sighed.

'You love him, don't you?' She didn't wait for an answer, which was probably as well. 'So you'd better do something, my girl, or Paula will be moving in here. Here, give me that, and go back to them.'

She seized the crumpled tablecloth that Louise was clutching, with both hands, and secured it with a sharp tug. Then she carried it off to the laundry room, leaving Louise standing in the hall at the bottom of the stairs.

The others hadn't come into the hall, so they had either gone along the terrace to the drawing room, or were sitting on the terrace as Paula had suggested. Louise and Tom had had nearly all their meals on the terrace. He had kissed her there, and she had thought she was falling in love.

She wondered if she could get out of going to Paula's cottage tomorrow. Lilian wouldn't understand her giving in so tamely; there might be quite a few pep talks by Lilian before she accepted that James would be going his own way, and more often than not without Louise.

It was happening as Louise had been warned it would. She had accepted the terms, she should have no complaints. But she was not at all sure that she could bear to watch.

But she went back into the empty dining room, then walked along the empty terrace. They were in the drawing room, she heard the voices and the laughter as she drew near, and she looked in on a scene that could have come out of a play. The background of the elegant room was dramatic enough, and Paula sat in a dark blue velvet armchair with the rest of the company grouped around her.

Well, they seemed to be grouped around her, she was the centre of it all, she was doing the talking, and Louise knew that she had been among this furniture and these people many times before, with James, of course.

James was mixing drinks at a side table. She wondered if he would say, 'Welcome home, darling,' to Paula later, when they were alone. Paula was at home, she couldn't have looked more confident and assured if Louise had never set eyes on James and Paula had married him.

Louise stood in the French window for a moment, but of course her entrance lacked the impact that Paula's had had. When Louise walked in it didn't hold up the talk for a moment. Some of them glanced towards her. James glanced, and Robert Gillian half rose from his chair. But Louise slipped in quickly and silently, sitting down right away, causing no fuss at all. Although if she had come in banging a tambourine she doubted if even that would have halted Paula's flow.

Paula and Helga and Ben were all in entertainment and that was what they mostly talked about, glittering star-spangled talk that should have been fascinating to listen to. Everybody seemed to be enjoying themselves. Lilian kept giving Louise encouraging little smiles that Louise dutifully returned, but she couldn't think of anything to say all evening long.

It was a long evening. Louise sat with an untouched glass beside her. She daren't drink it because she needed every scrap of self-control she could summon up, and at the moment she was managing to sit quietly, smiling.

Paula was so incredibly beautiful that it hurt to look at her, and although all the windows were open Louise felt stifled. She touched the back of her neck, rubbing the tense muscles that were aching.

This could go on for ever, she thought. We could sit here all night with Paula and James making love in the way they speak to each other and look at each other.

Paula was flirting outrageously and James was certainly not discouraging her. He sat near to her and she touched him, leaning across, stroking his face, putting fingertips on his arms, reaching for his hand when a joke was told, so that they seemed to share all the laughter.

When Lilian said, with a smothered yawn, around midnight, 'I'm sorry, but I really do think I'll have to be going to bed,' Louise could have kissed her for breaking up the party. Whatever happened between James and Paula now at least she wouldn't have to watch.

Paula said, in a husky voice full of promise, smiling up at James, 'Do I sleep here, or does someone run me back to my little cottage?' and Louise heard herself say,

'I'll drive you back.'

Paula gasped. Then, with her blue eyes like chips of ice, she spat viciously, 'You must be joking, you stupid little——'

There was a moment's shocked silence, as though violence had come out into the open, and Robert Gillian began to say, 'May I——?'

'Come on,' said James. 'Say goodnight.'

Paula smiled at him again, no vestige left of her venom. 'Goodnight,' she said gaily to them all. 'Goodnight, goodnight, and you're all coming to my cottage for the day tomorrow, aren't you?'

'Of course,' said James. He went out with her, and Louise found Lilian standing beside her.

'Hard as nails, that one,' said Lilian, 'a grabber.' She looked around as though waiting to see who might contradict her, but nobody did. They were all beginning to look a little sorry for Louise, who didn't want pity, who only wanted to get away.

'Goodnight,' she said. 'Sleep well, everybody.'

They said their goodnights and left her, and she poured a stiff whisky to take up to bed with her. If she drank that straight off it might drug her asleep. Robert's parting remark had been how oppressive the heat was and that they were overdue for a storm.

If there should be a thunderstorm Louise was convinced that she would never last out the night, that she had no reserves left; the last few hours had drained her hollow.

She crept into bed, with dry sobs racking her. She didn't drink the whisky. This was going to be the pattern of her life and somehow she had to meet it with her own resources. It was going to be infinitely harder than she had anticipated because she hadn't realised that she loved him so much.

She did love him. That was why she had married him. Deep inside her she had loved him and hoped that he would love her. Compared with that his money hadn't mattered at all. Even Tir Glyn had hardly mattered.

She had wanted Tom—James—they had to be one man. She was burned up with need of him, and to-night he had gone with Paula because he was Paula's lover, and jealousy was tearing her apart.

Tears came suddenly and she wept into her pillow in an abandonment of grief. She made no attempt to hold them back. There was no way she could have done. They were a torrent, blinding her, choking her, and at last exhausting her so that she slipped into deep black suffocating sleep.

She woke gasping for air, her temples throbbing, the pillow wet beneath her face, and as she opened her eyes the room was grotesquely lit by a flash of white lightning, and thunder crashed overhead.

The storm had come. It was here in the room with her, and she moaned and pressed her hands to her eyes, but she could see the lightning through her fingers and the thunder made her head ache almost unbearably.

Always, when there was a thunderstorm at night, she covered her head with bedclothes and lay sweating until it was over. But if she did that tonight she would suffocate. She could hardly breathe as it was. She reached out a hand for the glass of whisky and knew that if she swallowed any she would probably be sick.

She had always had this phobia, but never as badly as this. Not even when she was a child. And now she could remember that night in her aunt's home. It must have been very soon after her parents were killed, she had woken in a storm and run along the dark corridor to her aunt's room, hardly more than a baby, whimpering and seeking comfort.

Her aunt had sent her back. 'Don't be a baby,' she had said, and left Louise in the dark in the storm, closing the door. She had known then that now her mother and father were dead no one loved her or cared about her. There was no one in the world she could run to.

That was how she felt tonight, because James was with Paula, half crazy with loneliness. Maybe Tom was here. Tom would have comforted her. If there was a man in the room next to hers tonight it would be Tom. He wouldn't have stayed with Paula, he would have come back home.

She got out of bed, her hands over her ears, shrinking away from the lightning flashes, so that she stumbled into the dressing table, her hands shaking so that she could hardly turn the knob of the door.

The corridor was empty. Between the rolls of thunder there was utter silence and the room next to hers was going to be empty. She knew it was. She would knock on the door and nobody would answer, then she would open the door and there would be nobody there.

She knocked and waited and prayed, and the door opened. James was in the brown dressing gown and she whispered, 'I'm sorry, but I'm so scared, I'm so frightened. I can't bear it. Please!'

He put his arms around her and she clung to him. She was such a fool, and she was sorry she was such a fool. 'Hush,' he said, 'it's all right. You're safe, I'm here, hush now.'

No one had ever said that to her, except Tom, and this was Tom, and he wasn't with Paula.

He carried her like a child and laid her on the bed,

cradling her in his arms, rocking her, stroking her hair, telling her that nothing was going to hurt her.

Louise believed him. She breathed again, her face pressed into his shoulder, her lips against the cool brown skin. She kissed his shoulder and lifted her head and in a lightning flash saw his eyes, his mouth. She was starved for his mouth, she hungered for his kisses. 'Kiss me,' her lips framed. 'Love me.'

His hands were still gentle, but as he caressed her her entire body shivered as all she felt for him came flooding over her. He kissed her tenderly, then again and again in a rising sensual joy of physical delight, her ardour matching his, her passion as demanding and giving.

It was right. It was wonderful and beautiful, and she was warm and loved, and so safe and strong that the thunderstorm raged itself out while she slept in her husband's arms ...

She woke alone. She sat up in James' bed and put out a hand, although she could see there was no one there. The bedside clock said almost ten and she stayed where she was for a little while longer, wishing that he would come back, wishing that he had waited for her to wake. Or woken her. She hadn't wanted to wake alone this morning.

Then she went to her own room, washed and dressed, made up and went downstairs. The house sounded busy, there were people around; she passed Mrs Horabin and said, 'Good morning,' and asked, 'Are they all up?'

'Oh yes, madam,' said Mrs Horabin, as though everybody had been about since dawn, which was highly unlikely. But James and all his guests were in the breakfast room, and from the looks of the table they had almost finished their meal.

Louise coloured as they turned their heads as she

walked in. 'I overslept,' she apologised. 'I'm sorry.'

'It was a bad storm, wasn't it?' said Helga. 'I'm not keen on them myself,' and James explained,

'I told them the storm disturbed you and you had a restless night.'

He smiled at her, but it wasn't a smile with a secret message. It didn't make her laugh inside. She would have thought he would have come to her when she walked into the room, but he didn't, and she went to her chair and poured herself coffee.

Helga got up and said cheerfully, 'Right, I'll go and collect my swim suit. What time are we going?'

James consulted his watch. 'In about half an hour?'

'To Paula's cottage?' Louise's voice was soft, hardly audible.

'Yes,' said James as though the question was unnecessary because they all knew that was where they were going today.

But Louise had thought plans might have changed. She had thought that after last night Paula might not be included in their plans.

She stirred her coffee carefully, although she hadn't put in the sugar yet. She saw now that although last night had been a deeply emotional experience for her it must have meant very little to James, because for him it had changed nothing.

CHAPTER NINE

THEY went in two cars to Paula's cottage, Robert and Lilian with James and Louise, and the rest following. James led the way because James knew the way. That didn't mean to say he had known it before yesterday,

Louise tried to tell herself. He had taken Paula home last night, but he had been back in Tir Glyn when the thunderstorm woke her, although she didn't know what time that was. It could have been five o'clock in the morning for all she knew. He could have stayed with Paula most of the night, and she must *not* be jealous, because that way she could make a public fool of herself before the day was out.

In the front of the car James and Robert were talking business, and sitting beside Lilian Louise was silent most of the time. Lilian chattered cheerfully and Louise was grateful to her. Lilian understood.

After the thunderstorm the weather might at least have been unsettled so that a whole day spent on the beach wasn't such a good idea, but the sun was shining again and the sky was blue, and there was no excuse at all for going back to Tir Glyn. Once they reached the cottage they might be there till dusk, and another thing—beach wear was not Louise's favourite clothing. She wore one-piece swimsuits and cover-up jackets, because she was bony. And look who she was competing against. Paula Cavell, with her perfect body.

James turned off the road, driving down a little jetty, into another cliff-encircled cove. It was rather like the place where he had asked Louise to marry him, and that was understandable; they could only be a mile or two apart, on the same coastline. It was very pretty, very pleasant. And there was Paula, waiting.

There was only the cottage here, no other buildings. Perhaps it used to be a fisherman's home, or perhaps someone had built it to retire to. It was a square stone cottage, with shutters and door painted pale blue. A perfect holiday home, but it would be lonely here in the winter time, and rather scarey if the sea ever came right up, practically lapping your doorstep.

Louise was trying to keep her thoughts on things

like that because they were impersonal, feelings didn't come into them.

Paula was waiting. She had come through the blue door of the cottage, and she stood on the jetty in the briefest of sea-green bikinis. She might have been wearing strands of seaweed, and the warm breeze gently lifted her fair hair. Today she looked like the Little Mermaid, who exchanged her tail for beautiful legs, except that Paula was far from dumb, and there was no sweet sadness about her.

As the car doors opened she reached James and flung her arms around him. 'Welcome home,' she said, and James laughed and said,

'That's highly hospitable of you.'

Louise wished she could laugh too, and say something that would tell Paula she had seen the photograph in the dressing room and wasn't worried about it, and thought the idea of Paula using the same greeting here was quite amusing. But it wasn't funny, and she couldn't laugh.

The second car drew up and the rest of them spilled out. They had to see inside the cottage first, of course. Except for Robert and James, who went down the two steps at the end of the jetty, walking along the beach, still talking, still business presumably. And Lilian, who stayed outside in the sunshine.

There wasn't that much to see in the cottage. You stepped into a living room, in which there were three closed doors. One was the kitchen, Paula said; another a bathroom, and the third a staircase leading to two bedrooms.

The furniture in the living room was mostly pine: dresser, table, chairs; with a small chintz-covered settee and an easy chair. There were several flower prints on the walls in white-painted frames, but nothing that Louise had seen in Paula's flat, which had been altogether grander and more glamorous.

This didn't really look like Paula at all. It was attractive, and seemed to Louise like a small guest house, and she wondered if Paula had taken it just for a few weeks. There was no feel of permanency. Paula was probably here because James was near, not because she wanted to live in this cottage, and that was no surprise.

As Lilian had said she might still plan to move into Tir Glyn, and it could easily be done. She could be sleeping in that canopied bed in the master bedroom yet. Not alone either.

Louise would have no say in the matter, no say at all; but she could make pretty darned sure that she wasn't in the house at the same time. James' friends could make what they liked of that, but when Paula walked in, to stay for even one single night, Louise would walk out.

Helga was saying that the cottage was sweet, and so it was with the sun streaming in through the door and window, a lovely holiday hideaway.

'Don't you like it, Louise?' Paula asked in sugared tones, and Louise realised that she must have been frowning. She said,

'Very much, it's delightful,' and Paula gurgled,

'Well. I don't think I shall ask you to redecorate it for me, not after what happened last time. You came rather too expensive.' Marrying James, she meant, and Louise felt they must all be asking themselves what had possessed James when he chose her instead of Paula.

But he hadn't lost Paula. He had said it was all over, but it wasn't. Louise said quietly, 'Are you staying long enough for the place to need redecorating? It looks to me as though it's been done for the season. How long have you rented it for?'

'But I *love* it round here.' Paula's china blue eyes widened. 'I planned to live here, didn't I?'

'Not in this house,' said Louise, as Paula had said last night.

Helga and Ben and Rex edged out into the sunshine. Last night it had been quite entertaining when Paula had turned up, but they didn't want to witness an actual row between these two girls. Without James around that might get embarrassing, and they were sorry for Louise. They knew Paula.

'We both know this is temporary,' said Paula. 'We both know why James married you.'

Louise kept her lips closed tight. She wanted to get out, but Paula moved first, shutting the door, talking softly, almost hissing, 'He thought it would bring me running when I heard, but I never imagined he'd actually go through with it. I thought I was calling his bluff. He *was* bluffing too, but he's a stubborn devil, and now he's landed himself with you and serve him right if it costs him.'

Louise daren't speak. She daren't open her mouth, because if she did the voice coming out would be loud and angry. She had no idea what the words would be but, for the first time in her life, she wanted to shout at someone, to yell them down.

She turned towards the door that Paula had pointed out as 'kitchen' and Paula said, 'If you're looking for Mary Edmunds you've got a long way to go. I sacked her for letting you loose in Tir Glyn while James was there.'

'You *what*?' Louise wasn't shouting, she was croaking. 'But she didn't know. It wasn't her fault. You can't do that!'

'I can do anything,' said Paula, and she was so beautiful, even while she was looking malicious, that

Louise almost believed she could. But this was so unfair.

The door opened and Lilian walked in as Louise was gasping, 'You sacked Mary Edmunds because she let me start on the house a couple of weeks early? Well, that can't be legal, you won't get away with that.'

Paula looked at Lilian, and shrugged, then said silkily, 'Marrying James *has* gone to your head. You're not *that* important. Mary and I just decided to part, she got another job.'

'Where?' demanded Louise.

'I don't know.' Paula shrugged her bare shoulders again.

'Well, I intend to find out,' said Louise.

'Do you?' Paula went into the kitchen, calling, 'Give her my love,' and coming out carrying three green bottles. 'Try this, Lilian,' she said, 'but I'm not sure we should give Louise any. She seems over-excited already.'

Lilian put a hand through Louise's arm. 'Come on outside,' she said. 'The air's fresher.' She led Louise down the steps on to the beach, and a little way across the shingle before she said, 'It would be legal. Paula wouldn't sack anyone so that they could claim against her. She's had plenty of practice. She rarely keeps staff longer than a month or two, and then more often than not they give her notice.'

Mary Edmunds hadn't seemed very happy in her job, Louise recalled, and she was efficient and able to look after herself, and although what had happened in Tir Glyn must have infuriated Paula, and Mary must have caught the brunt of her fury, Mary would probably have left before long anyway.

'I don't really know the young woman,' said Lilian, 'but I did see her a couple of times and I wouldn't think she'd have any trouble finding another job.'

'Unless Paula gave her a bitchy reference.' Louise bit her lip and looked back on to the jetty, where Ben was drawing corks out of bottles and Helga and Paula were pouring wine into tumblers. 'Would you ask Robert if he could find out?' Louise asked. 'If I go to James Paula's going to say what she said when you walked in, that it's nothing to do with me. That could be why she told me, to get me feeling worried and guilty and all set to make a scene.'

'More than likely,' Lilian agreed, and smiled and patted Louise's arm. 'Why don't you take a swim? The water looks lovely and swimming's very relaxing.'

'Not for me.' Louise began to smile too. 'I can't swim.'

'In that case,' said Lilian, 'we'll both have a glass of that wine, and then we can always go for a walk.'

In the end it was Robert and Lilian who went off walking, and Louise sat on the rocks. There was buffet food brought out on to the beach. Paula apologised that the food wasn't better, it was all ready-cooked, but she said she had told her secretary she could have today off, and they knew that she couldn't cook a thing herself. Nobody cared. This was picnic weather, and this was a lovely cove. Another car came down and a family of five got out, but that was all.

Robert and Lilian went early, the rest took it easy. Helga and Paula were both in bikinis. Helga's skin was attractively brown, Paula's was a fairer tan, a very pale gold, smooth and glossy. She stayed close to James wherever he was. When he walked along the beach she walked too. When he sat down in the little group, of Helga and Ben and Rex and Louise, Paula sat down, and contrived to always be within touching distance of him.

Both the girls were actresses and beautiful, but Louise had rarely been more conscious of her own physical shortcomings. She was wearing a swim suit in a swirling coral and brown, and a short matching silky jacket, and if she had been left alone she would have kept on the jacket. But Paula drawled, 'Aren't you a teeny bit overdressed for a day like this?' The sun was beating down and Louise said,

'I burn rather than brown.'

'Use my oil,' Helga thought she was being helpful. 'It's very good. You won't burn if you use this.' She dug it out of a beach bag and offered it to James, and Louise thought—if he touches me I shall cry out. If he strokes me I shall burst into tears and say, 'Please let's go away from here,' and James will ask 'Why?'

She reached out. 'Thank you,' she said, and he put the sticky bottle into her hand, and Paula said,

'I'll try it when you're through,' smiling sidewards at him.

Louise rubbed the oil on herself, while Helga and Ben ran into the sea, splashing about like dolphins in the shallows, and swimming up and down not too far out. Rex was reading a paperback and from time to time watching seagulls and boats through a pair of binoculars. He probably found them restful after aeroplanes.

James said, 'Come for a swim?' and Louise said apologetically,

'I can't swim.'

'I'll teach you.'

She had visions of herself spluttering and splashing while Paula watched and said quickly, 'I'll try in a little swimming pool first, where I can touch the sides.'

'You can always paddle,' said Paula. While she and James swam out into the deep water.

'Yes,' said Louise, and screwed the top back on the sun-oil bottle and returned it to the beach bag. If Paula used it she would certainly ask James to rub it on for her and Louise wouldn't enjoy that spectacle, but Paula said, 'Come on then, let's swim,' and ran ahead as fast as the shingle underfoot would let her. The water looked deliciously cool, and Louise would have loved to plunge in, just to splash about and play like Helga and Ben had been doing, but she was afraid that she would look ridiculous.

'No?' said James, and she shook her head, smiling.

'No, thank you, I'm fine here. It's lovely.'

She watched the four of them, and then James and Paula swam away. She thought James went first, but she wasn't sure, and Paula was swimming almost beside him. With the sun on the water it wasn't easy to follow the heads of the swimmers. James' thick dark hair would be glistening wet, water falling away from his arms as he lifted them in the crawl stroke. Paula's hair would be floating out around her, her strokes would be graceful, less powerful, but they kept pace with each other, and Louise strained to watch until she wasn't sure whether she could see them or not.

They were a long way out, and she turned to Rex, who had put down his book, and asked, 'Can you see them?' He grinned.

'Don't worry. Paula's a good swimmer, and James is unsinkable. Here,' he offered her his binoculars and she put them to her eyes, fiddling with the adjuster until the picture cleared.

She found Helga first, vivid down to a little run in her mascara. They were very powerful glasses. Then she panned across the rippling water and her breath caught in an audible gasp as she saw James, seemingly as close as Helga had seemed.

He was speaking, she could see he was, and it felt odd that she couldn't hear him. She wished she could lip-read. No, she didn't. She didn't want to know what he was saying to Paula, when they thought that no one in the world could see or hear them.

She moved the glasses the merest fraction to find Paula. Her mascara hadn't run—if she was wearing any. The dark sweeping lashes could be natural, even with the blonde hair. Physically everything about Paula seemed just about perfect. She was laughing now, and in anyone else teeth as perfect as that would be capped, but they were probably Paula's own.

Well, there was no need to worry if they were safe out there. Safe from drowning, that is. They looked as though they could swim for miles in comfort, so Louise handed back the binoculars and said, 'Thank you. Isn't it incredible?'

'What's incredible?' Rex Hooper was a cheerful man, with a florid face and a ready grin.

Paula and James were incredible, everything about them; and Louise was feeling duller and more commonplace by the minute. She said, 'It's incredible how clearly you can see through these things. You could be out there, swimming. You can feel the spray on your face.'

'Yes.' But her chatter wasn't fooling him; perhaps she had given herself away by her expression while she had the binoculars to her eyes. 'You've made a first class job of Tir Glyn,' he said.

'Thank you.' She thought she had. It was a splendid house, but her designs had helped to make it that way and it was nice to know she had talent. Her days could always be busy, although the nights might destroy her.

'I've got a couple of rooms in my house that could do with a new image,' said Rex. 'I'd like your advice on them.'

'Of course. Where is it?'

'Marlborough.'

'Nice town. Tell me about them.'

She sat with her hands clasped around her knees,

and the smell of sun-oil in her nostrils, while he described two living rooms in his home. They sounded fine rooms, and she would be pleased to go down and suggest a change of image for him if that was what he wanted, so long as it was all he wanted and he wasn't hoping to cash in on a little consolation.

He was twice married and recently divorced, and he seemed nice enough and attractive enough, but he was leaning closer than necessary and smiling a little too knowingly. Somebody fancies me, she thought wryly, and knew it was unthinkable.

As soon as she could, without being offensively blunt, she stood up, and he asked, 'Where are you going?'

'Into the cottage. I thought I'd do the washing up.'

'Paula's got a girl, hasn't she?'

'She's got a secretary, who mightn't be thrilled to come back from her day off and find a kitchen full of dirty dishes. Besides, I want to freshen up.'

She gave him a polite little smile and walked away. She was hot and sticky, but the obvious place to freshen and cool off was in the sea, and she half expected him to call after her and point that out.

The picnic remains had all been dumped on the living room table, and Louise carried them into the kitchen. She didn't know why she should be doing this for Paula, but sitting in the hot sun so long was giving her a headache. Either the sun or the strain of having Paula around, and it was cooler in here.

She wished Robert and Lilian would come back, but they must have found somewhere to eat, and probably wouldn't turn up till it was time to return to Tir Glyn. They liked being together. They liked company, but they enjoyed each other's company best. Like Barbara and Alan. There were a lot of happy marriages. It wasn't true that marriage was dying. Marriage was alive and well and living in millions of homes, big and small.

If James had been Tom they might have had a home like this little cottage, and she would have been happy instead of bitterly unhappy. She had never been jealous before, and it was horrible. It twisted inside her like little knives. She had read that description of jealousy more than once, and it was true.

She looked out through the window, over the sands to the sea, but without the binoculars it was too dazzling to pick out the swimmers. By now they could be out of sight. Or they could have swum along the coastline and come ashore in another cove—a deserted one.

Louise could imagine them walking out of the water, Paula a sea nymph with her fair sleek dripping hair, and James gleaming like one of those bronze statuettes of Ancient Greek athletes. They would come out of the sea together, holding hands, and then turn to each other and walk higher up on to the lonely beach, his brown arm around her pale shoulders.

Louise's imagery shut off there, because this was no way to get through the day and the rest of her life. She'd have to keep her imagination in check if she was going to stay sane and sensible, and she was going to need a lot of sanity and sense.

She went into the kitchen again. There wasn't so much to do when the debris was disposed of and the dishes were stacked, and within ten minutes she had everything put neatly away.

She wondered about Paula's secretary, and then she wondered if there was a secretary down here. If Paula's object was James she wouldn't want another girl underfoot in this tiny cottage. She might have an employee lodging somewhere else—she'd said her secretary had brought her up to Tir Glyn last night, but when James drove her back home did they come to an empty house?

If Louise went upstairs would she find one bedroom or two occupied? Not that she was going to look. She hoped there was someone else here, but how much did it matter if Paula was all alone? She had a flat where she could entertain alone any time she chose. There were places all over the world where she and James could be undisturbed together.

The door opened and Rex walked in calling 'Louise, are you all right?' and she came out of the kitchen.

'Of course I'm all right, I've just been making myself useful and now I'm wondering about some coffee. Would you like some coffee?'

'Splendid,' he said. He sat down in the armchair to wait for it, and she put the kettle on a gas ring. Then she found some instant coffee, four mugs and two cups, and laid a tray; and went to stand at the open outer door waiting for the kettle to boil.

She hadn't thought about coffee until Rex walked in, but she wouldn't like him to know she had just been standing here brooding. Nor did she want to be shut in, talking to him. It would be awkward if he became too sympathetic.

James and Paula were out of the water and so were Helga and Ben. Helga was dabbing herself with a towel, Paula was sitting on a rock running her fingers through her hair, and James was looking around. When he saw Louise he waved and began to walk towards her, and Paula slithered off her rock and came too, tossing her head to dry her hair in the sunshine.

'Coffee's nearly ready,' said Louise, as they came up on to the little jetty. 'I hope you don't mind, Paula?'

'Mind?' echoed Paula. 'Why should I mind? I'd love a cup. And you've cleared up everything, how sweet of you.' Reaching the cottage, she said, 'Hello, Rex, have you been helping her? I wouldn't have thought you were so domesticated.'

'Oh, I can be very helpful,' Rex chuckled.

'I'll bet,' said Paula. 'You're not blushing, are you, Louise?' and Louise, who hadn't been blushing, felt the blood begin to burn in her cheeks. She was furious at herself, especially as James was smiling as though he was amused at her, and at Paula's teasing.

The kettle whistled and it was James who went into the kitchen and poured water on to the coffee, but Paula didn't tease him with being domesticated. Probably because Rex looked like a comfortable family man in that chintz armchair, while James had an untamed restlessness about him

By the time Lilian and Robert came back it was time to return to Tir Glyn. The weekend was over. Ben and Helga would be leaving after breakfast in the morning, and so would Lilian and Robert. Louise had thought James would be going on Monday morning too, and she was surprised to hear he had to be away tonight.

They were getting into the cars and Ben was yawning. 'I don't know about you,' he said to nobody in particular, 'but I'm worn out. It's all this exercise. Will anybody mind if I get into an armchair for the rest of the evening and stay there till bedtime?'

'That's what most of us will be doing,' said Robert, and grinned at James. 'Except you, of course.'

Louise hadn't known till then that James planned to leave tonight. 'Something came up' was his explanation, and everybody accepted it because with his multiple responsibilities something always was turning up. There was no hard and fast timetable for James, no nine-till-five and regular weekends off for him.

But Paula smiled secretly, catching Louise's eye.

Although she said goodbye to them all, and waved the cars off without mentioning any arrangements for future meetings. 'See you before too long,' she said, but Louise wondered what arrangements she and James had made when they were lonely swimmers, far out there in the bright water.

James wasted no time in Tir Glyn. They all went to their rooms when they got back. Louise took a bath, washing off the sun-tan oil and finding her skin much the same old colour. Perhaps a little pinker, which could have been the sun before she put on the oil.

She got dressed, and was sitting at the dressing table finishing her make-up, when there was a knock on the door. 'Come in!' she called.

James came in. He was wearing a lightweight beige suit, and an open-necked brown silk shirt. The familiar after-shave lotion reached her, and Louise picked up a perfume spray from her dressing table and applied a little to her wrists, sniffing at it. She didn't want to be reminded how James smelt, close to.

'I'm off now.' He bent to kiss her cheek and she sat very still. 'You'll be all right?' He sounded concerned about her, and he probably was.

'Of course I'll be all right,' she said. 'I've got plenty to do.' Tir Glyn was nearly finished, another two or three weeks would see it completed. She hadn't been working to a deadline. She had taken it leisurely because there had been other things to do: entertaining, putting on the act of being James' wife. She asked, 'When will you be back?'

'Next Sunday.'

'I see. By the way, Rex wants me to design a couple of rooms for him.'

'Good.'

Suppose she said, 'He's sorry for me. They're all sorry for me, but he fancies me. Perhaps he even prefers skinny women.' If she said that James would laugh. 'Goodbye then,' she said.

'Come and see me off,' he invited. For whose benefit? Ben's and Helga's. Surely not the Gillians'. Perhaps he didn't like to leave her sitting there alone. Perhaps he felt sorry for her too. She got up. 'All right,' she said.

He took the car and she waved him goodbye, just as Paula had done, but without Paula's smug little smile.

The helicopter was here, and it would have been quicker. He could have left by helicopter in the morning. Unless he was stopping on the way. Perhaps an overnight stay somewhere. Paula's cottage, perhaps.

Lilian met her as she turned back into the house and said, 'He works too hard, of course, but that's why he's where he is and who he is.'

'With a little help from the family firm,' said Louise drily.

'Not that much help,' said Lilian. 'It was small fry when James came into it.'

'Don't tell me he's a self-made man,' said Louise incredulously, and Lilian smiled,

'Yes, he is.'

It was nice of Lilian to stress that it was pressure of work that had taken James away tonight. If Louise could believe that she would be happier, but the nagging doubt that he was going to Paula persisted.

It was a quiet evening. With James gone the house seemed to lose its heart. Louise went on playing the hostess, and wished they would all pack up and go now instead of waiting till morning.

Even Lilian. If the house had been empty of guests she would have started work tonight. The staff would have thought she was mad, if the staff ever thought anything about her at all, but she had to wait until the guests had gone.

Next morning she came down to breakfast dressed

for work, and said goodbye to them all. She had hardly slept last night, thinking of James and Paula, but she would sleep tonight. She wouldn't stop working until she was ready to drop. If she kept at it non-stop she could finish here this week, and then start on the commissions that would take her away. She had to widen her horizons so that James was not the centre of her life, because she was such a tiny unimportant part of his.

Mrs Horabin came in about lunch. She had often seen Louise at work, this was nothing new; but when Louise said, 'Anything, a sandwich,' as she had lots of times before, this time Mrs Horabin said,

'A sandwich isn't going to keep you going.'

She knew that Paula was here on Saturday, of course, and where they went yesterday. She knew that James had left last night, and she probably had a shrewd idea of the situation. If she was trying to keep Louise going it sounded as though she was on Louise's side, and although she was backing a loser Louise appreciated this first show of concern. She smiled and said, 'Two sandwiches, then.'

When her lunch tray was brought in—by Mrs Horabin again—there was a bowl of soup on it as well as the plate of daintily cut sandwiches; and when it was dinner time Mrs Horabin put up quite a determined effort to get her to stop working.

But Louise wasn't weary enough yet. She wasn't risking another sleepless night. 'I've often worked a twelve-hour day,' she said, and took half an hour off for her meal, and then went back to her wallpaper stripping.

The phone rang several times that day. Lilian rang from home and Louise made herself sound cheery, she didn't want Lilian worrying. She didn't want Lilian interfering, although she couldn't think of anything

Lilian could do. She had her own plans, and the first was to complete Tir Glyn.

There were a couple of chat-calls, women who had been here, and were almost friends because Louise was married to James. She talked brightly to them too, and wondered if they had heard about Paula's cottage, and that Paula might well be with James now. He could have taken her up to London with him when he went. She had a script to learn, but she could learn that anywhere.

James rang during the evening, and Louise took the call on the upstairs phone in the master bedroom. This was the nearest phone to where she was working, and it hadn't mattered with the other calls, but speaking to James she was very aware of being in Paula's room. She felt what she was, an outsider, a girl with paint on her jeans and plaster dust in her hair.

She was suddenly tired, and her voice was flat and dull. Yes, she said, she was all right, but she had been working and she was tired.

'Don't overdo it,' he said.

'Nor you.' Not that he was ever tired. What was he doing tonight? Right now? Where was he, and who was with him? She said, 'There's no news. Nothing has happened since this morning, nothing's changed. Lilian phoned. They got home safely.'

'I know,' he said, 'I've seen Robert.'

'You see,' she said. 'There's no news, nothing to tell you.'

He suggested an early night. If she had done the same she would have had to add—'alone', and that would have made her sound waspy and jealous, so she said, 'Good idea, thank you for calling, goodnight.'

'Goodnight,' he said, and Louise thought she hung up first.

She went on working until it was very late. She got

up early and started again, and she kept up the pace all week. Mrs Horabin started clucking over her, becoming surprisingly human so that if Louise had had the time Mrs Horabin might have been prepared to talk about James.

That was ironic, because Louise no longer wanted to hear. She knew as much as she needed to know, including the fact that she was in love with him, and that she wanted him and would always want him. But every time she thought about him it hurt, and the last thing she needed was a chat about him with Mrs Horabin or anybody else.

Rex phoned—to thank her for the weekend, he said, and he would like to return her hospitality, and when could she come and look at those two rooms? She thanked him, and put his name well down the list of her future appointments.

She certainly wasn't starting an affair with anybody. She was a great deal more self-reliant than she had been before her marriage and she would never run to anyone again. Next time there was a thunderstorm she would put her head under the sheets, whether it suffocated her or not. James hadn't turned her away, as her aunt had done all those years ago, but he had rejected her just the same.

She planned her future, while she worked on the completion of Tir Glyn. She would keep her Northern office, and perhaps eventually open a London one. She phoned Barbara, and told her everything was wonderful. She was becoming an accomplished actress, or a good liar. She promised to drive up next week, and Barbara said she would round up her old friends and they'd have a get-together. 'You don't want me to invite Barry Mason, I suppose?' Barbara chuckled. 'I saw him the other day and he asked after you. He still doesn't seem able to get over your luck.'

'He's not the only one,' said Louise. 'Believe me.'

By Saturday she was on her second day in the last room. The little bedroom she had used when she first came up here, the one where one wall was to be covered with small scarlet hearts, and the white door panelled in scarlet.

She didn't know why she had left this till last, except that it was a room with memories. While she slept here she had thought James was Tom and begun to dream of a very different future. They had been good days. She wished...

She was impatient with herself, wasting time wishing, she wanted this room finished by night. When James came tomorrow she would be well groomed, dressed like a model. She had the clothes to dress like a model. He'd be surprised to see how much she had done, he'd phoned a couple of times and she'd said she was working, but he had no idea that she had finished it all.

She went at it feverishly. Mrs Horabin came and shook the ladder at one stage, while Louise was half way up it, and said, 'He told me to look after you. What's he going to say about you never stopping before midnight?'

'Very little, I should think,' said Louise. What James had probably said was, 'Look after things', and Mrs Horabin was concerned because Louise was looking rather a sketch. But as soon as this room was finished she would do a Cinderella and transform herself into the elegant mistress of Tir Glyn. She was looking forward to that. She would pretty herself, and put on one of her very best dresses. A swishing silky skirt would make a nice change after a week in working jeans.

When the phone rang she padded along to answer it, and took it again in the main bedroom. This time it was Paula, and she wished she had let someone downstairs take it so that they could have said she was busy and couldn't be disturbed. It was too late now.

'Hello, darling,' said Paula. 'I thought I'd let you know that I'm coming up to Tir Glyn next weekend, that's next Friday.'

'Are you?' said Louise grimly.

'Oh, I've been invited,' Paula purred. 'But I thought you might like a little warning. Perhaps you'd rather not be around.'

She had meant to be at Barbara's, she had promised herself she would never spend a night in this house while Paula was here, but she said, 'It doesn't worry me,' and Paula laughed.

'No? I thought it did. I'll see you then.'

Of course it worried her. It made her feel ill. She went back and tried to work, and tried to think of something else. Mary Edmunds did have another job, a good one. Lilian had phoned through to tell her, and given her Mary's address, and as soon as she had finished here she would write to Mary.

But she couldn't keep her mind from next weekend, when she knew that Paula would move into Tir Glyn as she had always meant to, as its mistress and as James' mistress. She was tired to death, she was worn out, and she couldn't be here, but wherever she was next weekend was going to break her.

She went on working for another half hour, for the first time in a long time getting things wrong, misjudging the pattern, feeling her eyes blurring and her hands shaking. It was late afternoon and she should stop. She could finish tomorrow before James came, or she could make herself more presentable so that it wouldn't matter if he came before she had finished.

Although what did it matter what she looked like, when Paula was moving in next weekend? She sat on the top platform of the ladder and stared at the red hearts on the wall opposite, and felt a red rage against Paula and James, who must believe she was the door-mat to end all doormats.

Fury, combined with fatigue, was a heady brew. There was a half empty tin of red paint down there, and if she could have reached it by stretching she would have hurled it at the wall. When the door opened she turned, glaring, and the fact that it was James and not Mrs Horabin only deepened her scowl.

He looked up at her and asked, 'What the hell are you doing? You look terrible.'

'You weren't supposed to be here till tomorrow.' Louise hardly recognised her own voice, it was so harsh. 'And what the hell does it matter how I look? I'm working, aren't I? Finishing this place.'

'What's the rush?'

That was a reasonable question, but she said sav-agely, 'We want it nice for Paula's visit. She hasn't seen over it, not since just before we moved in, so now she can look around and be proud of it. By the way, do you mind if I invite Rex over next weekend?'

'Yes, I do,' said James.

'I suppose it would be handier for all if I went to his place.'

He began to smile. She watched him, and he said, 'If you go looking like that I should think he'll send you right back again.'

The laughter did it. She was not only a doormat, she was a joke. They laughed about her, and she shouted wildly at him, 'You can have the house to yourself any time you want, bring anybody you want here! Just let me finish this room because I wouldn't like to leave it in this state, I do have some professional pride left. I wasn't expecting you back yet—are you staying or are you on your way to the cottage?'

She had to stop for breath and he said, 'For a girl

who can't stand shouting you've got a good voice there.'

And then he went, closing the door, and at the sound of the quiet click the anger drained out of her. All the heat of the moment had gone and she was very cold. He had gone, and she knew he was going to Paula, in the car, and he mustn't go in the car.

She jumped off the ladder and ran down the back stairs, but the car wasn't at the back of the house, and by the time she had made a dash through the hall to the front door he was sitting in the driver's seat.

Louise called 'Wait, please!' and fled down the stone steps. James opened the car door as she reached him and she gasped, 'Don't go in the car. Walk away if you've got to, but please don't go in the car.'

'Why not?' He thought she'd flipped, she must sound as though she had. She croaked,

'I know it's crazy, but I know why I'm scared of rows—shouting. I just suddenly know.'

He got out of the car and took her hand, and sat down on the steps pulling her down beside him, as they had sat together in the very beginning. 'So tell me,' he said.

'There was a row before my parents died.' She crossed her arms and sat, hunched. 'I don't think there were many, I'm almost sure we were all happy together, but I know there was shouting the night they—never came back. I've never shouted since, I've never yelled at anyone.'

It was ridiculous. You couldn't kill by raising your voice, although at four years of age the quarrel and the tragedy must have seemed part of the same nightmare.

She whispered, 'Sorry, I'm tired, it makes me stupid. I've finished the house.'

He said gently, 'You look as though the house has nearly finished you. Come on.' With an arm around her he helped her up the steps, guided her into the drawing room, and sat her down in a deep soft armchair. He sat down himself and she asked,

'Are you going to Paula's tonight?'

'No.'

'No?' She wasn't clutching at straws, she knew how the land lay. She said, in an offhand manner, 'Oh well, she's coming here next weekend, isn't she? She phoned about an hour ago and told me she'd been invited.'

'Then she invited herself,' said James, and Louise squeaked,

'You didn't?'

'No.'

She sat up in her chair, asking the question she was terrified to ask. 'You are her lover, aren't you?'

'I'm your lover.' He looked straight at her and hoped flared in her. She stammered,

'But this set-up, this marriage, it isn't a real marriage. You asked me to marry you because—you said——'

He said quietly, 'I asked you to marry me because I wanted to take care of you, and I'd just seen Paula's idea of a marriage settlement.'

So Paula had been too greedy, a grabber who grabbed too soon. After that Louise was probably a bargain, and she smiled a little because that could be a beginning.

'Was that why you quarrelled?' she asked.

'It sparked off the discussion,' said James drily. 'I can buy most things and I expect to pay. But I suddenly realised that I didn't want to buy a bride, and I didn't want Paula for my wife at any price. I thought you thought I didn't have a penny to my name.'

'I did, until——'

'You knew who I was before I told you.' He smiled at her, affectionately she hoped, and she asked,

'How did you know that?'

'Mason was drinking in the hotel I was staying in, the night I took you back to your flat.' The night he had said he would see her next morning but had sent her a letter instead. He hadn't seen her again until they met and married. He went on, 'He told me he'd phoned here and you'd discussed me. He said you'd walked out on him because his prospects were rocky but you should be having better luck with me.'

That sounded like Barry. He'd get all that into one self-pitying whine. James wouldn't have to hang around to hear it, and she was sure he hadn't. James had a poker face when he needed it. Barry would never realise what he was telling him.

She said, 'I didn't know until Barry rang me, and I don't think I really believed him. Did you think I was marrying you for your money?'

'It seemed likely.' She had thought so once herself, but she had been wrong. She had married for love.

'So why did you go through with it?' she asked, and he said,

'I told you. I needed a wife around, I didn't want anyone else pestering me to marry them.'

'Oh!' Her heart sank.

'And because I loved you,' he said. 'Because I wanted you at any price.'

His need and his yearning for her were in his face, and she cried out against whatever it was that had kept them apart. 'Then why, *why*, that first night in Paris——?'

'You didn't seem to want me.'

'I was scared.'

'So was I.'

'I don't believe you.' He was a man who took compliance for granted, arrogantly self-assured, but now he sounded as vulnerable as a boy in love.

'I daren't make love to you in case you drew back,' he said huskily. 'I was half crazy for you, but I didn't think you wanted me. Even after the thunderstorm I was scared to face you next morning. You're a cool lady. I hoped you'd come across to me when you came into that room, but you didn't.'

Louise held out both hands to him. 'I was thinking you might have come across and kissed me.'

He came across then and lifted her to her feet and kissed her on the mouth and held her for a long time, and she knew that she would never be afraid again, of anyone or anything.

She smiled as she admitted, 'I was jealous of Paula.' His arms were still around her as though he would never let her go, and he smiled too.

'I didn't know she was walking in last weekend, but even Paula has her uses. I could have been very jealous of Rex.'

'Could you?' Louise opened wide dancing eyes. 'What about all that talk that I could do what I liked so long as I told you?'

He kissed her again, lightly this time, on the tip of the nose. 'So long as I knew I could have broken it up, couldn't I?' and she laughed and shook her head and said,

'What a two-faced character I've married! What about next weekend? Shall we invite them both down?'

He shrugged, 'Why not? We'll be away. That's why I've been working non-stop since last Sunday night, so that I could have this week clear for that honeymoon we never had. I thought I'd take you to an island tomorrow. I've got some gen in the car, I'd gone back to fetch it.'

'I'd like that, I'd love that.' She looked down at herself. 'What a sight I look! I need a bath, I must get cleaned up.'

'Then an early night for you,' he said.

'But I'm not tired any more.'

He slid his hands slowly down her back, round her waist, drawing her against him again, asking, 'Who said anything about sleeping?'

YOUR LOVE-NATURE
WATER SIGN   **February 20-March 20**

Your Pisces love-nature is highly emotional, affectionate, sentimental, giving and self-sacrificing. You are unhappy without someone to love; but, on the other hand, you can be equally unhappy when you are in love. Sensitive and emotionally insecure, jealous and possessive, subject to frequent moods of depression and morbid gloom, you are easily hurt by a careless word or any hint that your lover is not completely faithful. Because of this sensitivity, it is important that you choose your romantic partners wisely.

When involved in a relationship you are totally committed; you are content to be alone with your lover, the rest of the world shut out. While you enjoy the physical side of love, you expect more from sex than sensual enjoyment; ideally it should be the sharing of a deep spiritual communion. This depth of sharing is hard to reach, but you persist, optimistic that the ideal relationship can eventually be worked out. You are happiest when doing things for others and you melt at the thought that someone needs you. Then your ready sympathies overflow; you are willing to sacrifice, tolerate, forgive—in short, to give your all for love.

Your best mates are found in the other water signs, Cancer and Scorpio, who understand your sensitivities but are more worldly wise. With another Pisces you can share everything, but there is a danger that the negative qualities will predominate. Earth signs are good partners also— they are stable, and their practicality helps shield you from the harsh realities of life.

And there's still *more* love in

Harlequin Presents...

Do you have a favorite
Harlequin author?
Then here is an
opportunity you must
not miss!

HARLEQUIN OMNIBUS

Each volume contains
3 full-length compelling
romances by one author.
Almost **600** pages of
the very best in romantic
fiction for only **$2.75**

A wonderful way to collect
the novels by the Harlequin
writers you love best!